WHEN A MAN LOVES A WOMAN 4/04

The baron barred her way, touching her chin lightly with his finger. He gazed down at her with an intensity she found unnerving. "You deserve a man who is devoted to you. He should not look kindly on you spending hours with me. I could kiss you and would he care? I doubt it."

As though to demonstrate his point, he gathered a bemused Tabitha in his arms. He placed his lips lightly on hers in what was probably intended to be a slight touching of lips to make his point.

Only it didn't work out that way.

Tabitha felt as though she were aflame. A fire singed her nerves, tingled through her veins, melted her spine. She responded like a bird soaring to the sky for the first time, hesitant, then gaining power, and finally exultant at the flight that had been achieved. She had longed for this and yet had not known it. . . .

Tabitha's Tangle

Emily Hendrickson

A SIGNET BOOK

FεC

308- 4053

SIGNET
Published by New American Library, a division of
Penguin Group (USA) Inc., 375 Hudson Street,
New York, New York 10014, U.S.A.
Penguin Books Ltd, 80 Strand,
London WC2R 0RL, England
Penguin Books Australia Ltd, 250 Camberwell Road,
Camberwell, Victoria 3124, Australia
Penguin Books Canada Ltd, 10 Alcorn Avenue,
Toronto, Ontario, Canada M4V 3B2
Penguin Books (N.Z.) Ltd, Cnr Rosedale and Airborne Roads,
Albany, Auckland 1310, New Zealand

Penguin Books Ltd, Registered Offices:
80 Strand, London WC2R 0RL, England

First published by Signet, an imprint of New American Library,
a division of Penguin Group (USA) Inc.

First Printing, March 2004
10 9 8 7 6 5 4 3 2 1

Chapter One

The young woman summoned to the library couldn't have been far away, for she appeared at once in response to her father's request. Her gaze was questioning, but she merely said, "You wished to see me, Papa?"

"Tabitha," the rector intoned in his kindly manner, "Baron Latham has a project to place before you. He would like your assistance to catalogue a collection of books he has acquired. I expect you will be only too pleased to assist him." There was no question in his voice. He assumed she would do as suggested without hesitation.

Hugh, Lord Latham, watched as Tabitha Herbert stood meekly before her father, listening to the proposal offered her. She had placed her hands behind her, but her chin tilted upward as if in challenge. The light from a window gave Hugh a good look at her porcelain skin, sweetly curved lips, and soft blue eyes that flashed with hidden thoughts. The sun picked out highlights in her silver gilt hair. He'd never seen hair so unusual and beautiful. What, he wondered, was going on behind those glittering eyes? His only interest in her was her ability—should she actually have such. His hopes were not terribly high.

Tabitha clenched her hands behind her. She dared not look at Baron Latham—the Black Baron! She was being offered a position to catalogue his acquisition of books, nothing more perilous. Merely because she thought the baron aloof and too conscious of his title was no reason to deny herself the pleasure of dealing with his books. His dark hair and eyes had made him seem somewhat sinister, especially with his air of reserve. Now he appeared almost cordial. He was not at all like his former neighbor, the late Baron Rothson.

Clearly Baron Latham couldn't find a man to do the job or she would never have been asked. She loved handling books. To have access to a great collection was more than she had ever anticipated coming her way. If she chanced to glance at him, he would see the gleam of hope in her eyes. It might be as well if he thought she was doing him a favor—perhaps even reluctantly. She was meticulous in her care. Working for him would not be easy; he would demand much.

Little had she dreamed that her penchant for reading would bring her into the proximity of the man she'd dubbed the Black Baron. He was a mystery, his dark eyes revealing nothing. Yet he was a polished gentleman, one to admire.

She had watched from a distance as he had added to his home—wings to either side of the central block. It was said that one wing was a picture gallery, the other a library. She didn't care much about the pictures, but she ached to have access to that vast library. And now she could!

"I would be pleased to assist the baron with his books." She was surprised at how calm she sounded, quite as though she was agreeing to help with something ordinary.

"How soon could you come?"

Tabitha pretended to consider the matter. "I could come tomorrow if it is agreeable with my father." She glanced at Papa, not the least surprised at his answering nod. The baron had contributed handsomely to the new roof on the church and Papa appreciated his support.

The baron rose from his chair by the fire, said all that was proper, casually informing Tabitha what time she would report come the morning, and left the room, brushing past Tabitha with a tantalizing trace of scent.

Crossing to the window, she watched him mount his splendid black horse, then canter down the drive. His estate stood at the far end of Rustcombe. While Tabitha didn't disdain his vast and beautiful park and the handsome buildings, it was the man who intrigued her. What went on in his head? What thoughts lurked behind his dark eyes?

He was a tall, dark, romantic figure, the dashing sort of man Tabitha often daydreamed about. Her sisters teased her about her fanciful notions, laughing with sisterly affection at her love for dramatic tales and Byronic heroes. The Black Baron had often figured in her dreams.

The following morning she was ready to leave the rectory far too early. Her mother examined her appearance with a tolerant eye while Tabitha fiddled with the neat white bundle she carried.

"I see you are being sensible. While that is not a dress you might wear to tea, it will do for unpacking books, I dare say." She met Tabitha's hesitant gaze.

"I shall put my apron on once I am in the new library." Tabitha held up the small white bundle for her mother to see. "I fear I cannot spare any dresses."

"We shall be able to afford several new gowns for you, my dear. It will not do for you to be seen at the baron's home looking like a servant!"

"Well, I suppose I might be considered in the light of one, you know. I have no illusions, Mama. Just because my sister has married exceedingly well does not mean I nurse ambitions to marry the baron."

"What will be, will be, dear child."

"Mama, I am nearing twenty years of age." Tabitha smiled fondly at her mother. It must seem odd to her that only her youngest remained at home when merely months ago the house was full of feminine chatter. Even her brother Adam stayed away, enjoying an end to his studies. He said he wanted to look around his father's ancestral village, perhaps even meet the famous Earl of Stanwell.

"I wonder if I shall eat luncheon alone, and where?"

"While I have it on good authority that Baron Latham has no more than seven and twenty years to his dish, I am quite certain he will have better manners than to allow that. Perhaps he may wish to consult with you regarding the arrangement of the books?" Mrs. Herbert eyed her daughter with speculation and not a little hope in her gaze.

"It is far more likely that I will have need to consult with him, and only about the books." Tabitha's voice and manner was dry, as was her mouth. Her nerves, while usually strong, were on edge. "Best not to nurture any hopes, dear Mama. I doubt the baron has the faintest of matrimonial thoughts in his head. If he does, they would be far more likely to go in the direction of Lady Susan Booth." With this Tabitha turned to stare out of the front window in the direction of the road.

"True." Mrs. Herbert had to acknowledge the reality of that remark. But she did so with a regretful sigh. Lady Susan was the daughter of an earl. She was lively and pretty, and her father's land marched with the baron's property on the far side. She was the most appropriate candidate for his wife.

The baron had said he would send a carriage for Tabitha, knowing it likely the rector would probably need his. There was as yet no sign of any vehicle. She would have to make it clear that she intended to be at work early in the day, not waiting until noon!

"I intend to ask the mantua-maker to bring a selection of fabrics over. You do need at least two new dresses."

Tabitha gave her parent a fond smile. "I think a nice greenish-blue, perhaps a yellow like moonlight, or I should think a lovely plum India mull would be nice."

"I shall see what may be had. I do not expect much, but we have some lace left from what your sister sent. I trust you will be at hand for fittings at the very least?"

Tabitha nodded. "Evenings free, for certain. I doubt I would ever work late—the light, you know. And weekends as well. The baron always attends church."

The smart curricle that turned into the rectory drive was *not* being driven by a groom. Baron Latham handled the reins with expert ease. She had not anticipated that *he* would come for her, and in his dashing new curricle!

Darting an anxious look at her mother, Tabitha made her way to the entry hall. She would not keep her new employer waiting. She opened the door, prepared to leave at once, only to be foiled. He nodded, then brushed past her to stride across the hall to where her mother stood.

He bowed over her mother's hand before saying, "I

wish to be clear that Miss Herbert will have a woman around her at all times. There is no danger of her being compromised while in my house, ma'am." A faint smile curved his lips.

"I expected nothing less, my lord," Mrs. Herbert said in a practical voice and manner.

Tabitha was glad that her parents had become so accustomed to dealing with titled people that a mere baron had no power to overset them. Nothing would be worse than to have a parent fawning over a gentleman who was inclined to be as reserved as Baron Latham.

He turned to Tabitha. "If you are ready to leave?" He gestured gracefully to the open door beyond which awaited his curricle.

Tabitha nodded and marched ahead of him, keeping her thoughts to herself. But for him to act as though she kept him waiting when it had been his notion to assure her mother that all would be proper was so much nonsense.

Accepting his hand, she climbed into the curricle, then sat with demure patience while he strode around to join her. She said not a word. If he was going to be so pompous, so top-of-the-trees, she had nothing to say.

They rode along in silence, with only the sound of the horse clopping on the hard road and the jingle of the harness to disturb their peace.

Hugh was thankful to have recalled that the rector or his wife would wish to be assured their daughter would be quite safe in his house. He wouldn't have had that worry if a man were coming to catalogue his books. This entire business was becoming fraught with implications he had not heretofore considered, one of which was her beauty.

It was Crowder who had murmured a few words to

reassure the baron that all proprieties must be observed. The raising of his butler's wispy brows and the meek folding of hands across his portly form reminded Hugh as nothing else might of what was due the rector's daughter.

Crowder had remarked upon the excellence of the rector's connections as the nephew of the Earl of Stanwell. She was of fine gentry, not some nonentity.

Still, the young woman at his side exhibited no signs of coquetry, indeed, none in the least. The thought that he might not merit such irritated him for a moment, then he sensibly decided that she might truly be bookish and not inclined to flirtatious nonsense.

"What have you read of late?" he inquired in a manner to depress any thoughts of charm had she cherished such.

"I read a travel guide to Switzerland. The Countess of Stanhope lent it to me. She supplements my reading, you see. Papa tends to buy very learned tomes. They might be uplifting, but a novel occupies the time more agreeably. I enjoy novels. Have you read *Pride and Prejudice*?"

Hugh admitted he had not had the pleasure. He thought he might look into the book, however. If the rector's girl thought it worthwhile, perhaps it might be of interest.

"You are interested in travel?" he inquired, turning to a safe topic. Somehow novels spelled danger.

The topic of world travel and where they might like to venture occupied them until they turned up the grand avenue that wound through the well-landscaped park to the house.

Tabitha gave the noble house an admiring look. The new ells gave it a grand appearance. Stately columns added to this look, as did the fine stone and splendid set of steps. She waited while a groom ran to stand

by the horse while the baron strolled to her side of the
curricle to assist her. She thought it quite handsome of
him when he might have turned her over to a servant
without a qualm.

The stout butler opened the front door in a rather
majestic manner. She had seen him at the rear of the
church after services so she happily nodded to him
and inquired how he was in her usual manner.

"This is Crowder. He will take care of anything you
may need." The baron sounded disapproving of her
geniality.

So, Tabitha thought, she had been right. She would
see little of the elusive baron. Well, it was fine with
her. She did not need the distraction he was sure to
offer.

She was escorted into what appeared to be a music
room to their left, then on through to the vast library beyond.

The library smelled faintly of paint and newly laid
carpet. There was an imposing walnut desk at the far
end of the room, situated so the person who sat there
might have the satisfaction of surveying the room's
entire contents.

Tall, many-paned windows were set between the
book stacks. Several of them appeared to be doors,
opening onto the terrace. She approved of the crisp
white paint on the shelves, so easy to keep clean. A
vast number of wooden crates littered the fine multi-
colored Axminster carpet.

"I shall leave you to begin as you see fit." The
baron bowed with exquisite manners, then disappeared the way they had entered, leaving her to stare
at the unopened crates.

Tabitha took a deep breath before turning to
Crowder. "Could someone help me pry the lids from
the crates? I question whether I could attempt it."

"Naturally, Miss Herbert." He sailed from the room to return shortly with a small, spare little man who had a pry bar in hand. In short order Price, as he was introduced, had all the crates opened and ready for her.

It was then the enormity of her project really hit her. There were hundreds and hundreds of books in those crates. Maybe over a thousand! Could she use the system she had used for her father?

"Oh, dear me." Her softly spoken words fell into the silence of the room like omens of doom. "Well," she said briskly, "the first thing is to unpack them all, then sort by author and topic. Following that . . ." She gave a frowning look at the many crates and the modest collection of books that were already on the shelves. "Well, I shall cross that bridge when I get there. If I ever do," she concluded with less optimism than she had felt yesterday.

A plump little maid slipped inside the door, seating herself on a wooden chair while trying to look unobtrusive.

Tabitha glanced at her, then realized this must be what the baron meant when he told Mama that Tabitha would be chaperoned. "You may as well make yourself useful if he thinks you ought to be in here," Tabitha said dryly.

"Yes, miss." The maid cautiously made her way around the crates of books, giving them the awe and respect that a reliquary would deserve.

"I want you to take the books from this crate one at a time, and hand them to me. I will begin to create piles according to my system." She didn't need to explain her system. Indeed, she wasn't entirely certain *what* system she would end up using.

Meow. The sound came from the open door, causing Tabitha to pause. She turned to see a handsome cat.

Suspicious green eyes stared at Tabitha with mistrust. Its gray and white fur fluffed out as it took exception to the intrusion of a stranger into its domain.

"That be Septimus, his lordship's cat."

"I daresay it was the seventh kitten?" Tabitha gave up her attempt at humor when the maid gave her a blank look.

"Well, I be told peers do favor odd names."

The cat wound its way carefully around the various crates until it reached Tabitha.

She gazed down at it, somewhat unnerved by the unblinking green gaze. "Good morning, Septimus. I trust you shall not find any mice in these crates. That is, if you deign to hunt for such creatures."

"That be the kitchen cat what hunts for mice."

Tabitha half smiled. "Somehow that doesn't surprise me, given his expression of lofty disdain."

The cat settled down precisely where Tabitha wished to walk, necessitating a detour to the other side of a crate, now half unpacked.

They kept at it at a steady pace. But when Crowder entered to request that Miss Herbert follow him to have her nuncheon, only one crate had been emptied, a second barely begun. Clearly, this would take longer than she expected.

Tabitha removed her white muslin apron, smoothed her hair, and then followed the portly butler. He led her along the central hall to a charming yellow dining room.

The baron stood by the window, staring out at the view beyond. Tabitha glanced out of the window to note that no flowers were to be seen, only a great variety of shrubbery and trees. A masculine scene, to be sure.

"It is a soothing view, is it not? Every shade and tint of green imaginable as far as you can see." Tabitha gave him a hesitant smile, not wishing to seem forward, but wanting to be at least mildly friendly.

His turn was abrupt and he looked at her as though he couldn't quite place her for a moment.

Tabitha suppressed a grimace. "I beg your pardon. Crowder said that nuncheon was to be served." She stood her ground, refusing to retreat from this intriguing and somewhat intimidating gentleman.

The baron cleared his throat, then gestured to a simple chair. The unpretentious table sat near the windows, decked in crisp white linen with attractive china set for two. Tabitha was not to eat alone—at least not today.

"Tell me how you go on," he invited after seating her, seeming to unbend a little, his dark eyes hooded.

"I do not imagine I have to tell you that there are an enormous number of books in those crates." Her words were cautious, not wanting to receive that blank look again.

"I suppose so," he answered politely. "I was not given a count. I trust all the books I purchased were delivered." He spoke with the assurance of one who was accustomed to being treated with all due deference.

"Perhaps there is an inventory list in one of them?" She hoped there was. It might give her an idea how the previous owner had arranged them on his shelves.

"I'd not thought of that. Let me know if you come across one, will you?" He spoke absently, as though his thoughts were elsewhere. Yet, he watched her.

Tabitha assured him she would do precisely that, then fell silent as Crowder and his minions served a light but delicious meal. If this was a sample of his nuncheons, it was unlikely he would become fat. The clear soup had a delicate flavor she found pleasing, while the rest of the meal was an equally subtle blending of tastes and textures. The baron was definitely a man of discriminating taste.

She didn't venture into another attempt at conversation. There appeared to be a gulf between them that would be difficult to bridge. If a gentleman had come to do this work, they would likely have had something to discuss.

"You like gardens?" he inquired, again rather abrupt.

"I do. Although, I confess I like flowers better than shrubbery. Do you have any topiary? I have seen a few and admire them. That would fit in with your shrubbery."

"You know, I have seriously thought of attempting a topiary garden. What do you suggest I have done first?"

Tabitha glanced down to where Septimus sat by the window, looking quite as aloof as his master. "A cat?"

"A crouching cat or one sitting up?"

"One of each," she said with an impish manner.

He also looked to where the cat sat and grinned. Tabitha was stunned at the charm of that grin. He became a different person when he smiled.

He smoothed his expression to one of politeness and replied, "I shall have a worthy model at any rate."

"What happened to the other kittens—seeing that Septimus is the seventh."

"Primus is now the kitchen cat, being—I am told—an excellent mouser. The others found homes elsewhere."

"I'm glad. Septimus seems a proper cat for a lord, being rather lordly himself." She had spoken without consideration for her choice of words. When he withdrew she scolded herself for her lack of tact. Apparently what she had said was wrong. Well, she could scarce apologize, for she thought her sentiment quite acceptable.

The baron smiled, albeit a bit restrained. "I imagine you are right. Now, I have an appointment with my bailiff so if you will excuse me?"

"Naturally." She turned in her chair to watch him leave the room, his tall figure rapidly disappearing.

Once alone, she consumed her pudding while deep in thought. "This will never do, my girl," she admonished. "It would be far better were you to eat alone by the books than disturb his peace." And hers as well!

Hugh strode along the hall to the rear of the house, then down the stairs to the small office where he met with his bailiff. He was early, so he stared out at the green view, wondering if he ought to attempt a topiary. She thought a cat to begin. He was trying to maintain a proper distance, but the appealing young woman didn't make it easy. He would strive to keep busy.

Although—he supposed he ought to check on her at least once a day? He nodded, satisfied he had the answer before turning to greet Jamison as he entered.

"Jamison, what do you think of doing a topiary?"

Chapter Two

Little by little the books were taken from the sturdy crates to be placed in neat piles around the edge of the room. Tabitha thought that it might be a clever idea if she suggested his lordship put a letter of the alphabet at the top of each section. There were only nineteen sections, but the letters Q as well as X, Y, and Z would have few volumes. That is, of course, if he agreed to have the books arranged by author. Unless he preferred to have authors alphabetized under topic headings. Books on botany, politics, and history were abundant. He appeared to have the latest releases in his own collection. She really ought to ask him what he preferred. It was unlikely he would not have an opinion on the matter. He was a decisive person.

About the time she prepared to leave the house, Lord Latham came into the library. He looked at the few empty crates, then at the vast number of remaining ones.

"I can see you are dismayed, sir." Tabitha rose from where she had been kneeling to sort through books.

"It will take longer than I thought." He turned to Tabitha and she paused while draping her shawl about her.

"I am quite careful. I'd not wish to harm any of these valuable books. I expect it will take me an entire week just to unpack them." She gave him a rueful smile. Septimus popped up from where he had been lounging and meowed.

The baron made a dismissing motion with his hand. "I know that anyone who enjoys reading and books will not be careless." He ran a finger around the inside of his collar while strolling over to gaze out of the window to view his grounds, looking on edge about something. He cleared his throat. "I spoke to my bailiff about a topiary. I thought perhaps I might try one to see how it goes."

She dusted off her hands, then folded up her apron before joining him by the window to speculate where he might put such a thing. "A green cat would assuredly add something to the landscape." She glanced at the animal that had joined its master to gaze out at the scene beyond.

He nodded. "I think a cat might be simple to begin. Don't you?" He stood with his hands behind him as though restraining them from doing else. "A crouching cat, looking about to pounce? Something like Septimus, I daresay?"

"Yes." Tabitha wondered why he had decided to create a topiary. And a cat, at that, although Septimus was worthy.

They stood in silence for a time. Tabitha found it disquieting. Unsettling. "I had best be going." She took a step from his side toward the doorway.

"It is that time of day. Growing late, that is. I'll send a carriage for you in the morning."

Hugh walked along with Miss Herbert to the large entry hall where he waited until the carriage appeared. Ignoring the groom waiting to assist her he personally saw to her comfort in the neat curricle, liking the feel of her small capable hand in his. She was lovely as well as clever.

The dust from the departing vehicle drifted away from the avenue, yet he remained, watching until it was out of sight. What had taken possession of him? Surely he had no interest in this young woman? Miss Herbert proved to be more than capable for the job, handling the books with proper regard. She was not a potential baroness.

Yet he had wanted to linger in the library to watch her. It was utter nonsense, of course. It had nothing to do with his cat, either. He grinned down at the animal that persisted in winding around his legs.

"Disgusting toady." Hugh studied his cat while he thought. The Earl of Montfort had made it clear that he would welcome Hugh as a husband for Lady Susan, the earl's daughter. She was a lovely young woman who would likely make a satisfactory baroness. Hugh was surprised that the earl didn't look higher—but then, Hugh's fortune compensated for his having a lower rank. That, and that their lands marched together on one side. Since Susan was an only child, it might please the earl to know that his acreage would be enlarged, and by a man who managed his own property well. And Hugh was, if nothing else, a good manager of his property even if his bailiff oversaw the application of most everything.

Hugh acknowledged no affection for that young lady. He felt nothing more than a polite interest—if that. She was more than eligible to be his wife. And he supposed he ought to be looking for such. He was not getting any younger—witness his approaching birthday, eight and twenty years he would be. The time rushed past far too quickly.

Turning to wander around the side of his house, he stared off across his parkland. He wondered if Miss

Herbert had seen his lake at its best. He thought she would enjoy watching the swans. Although—he had heard something about the old cob being a trifle aggressive. That was utter nonsense, most likely. At his side, Septimus surveyed the scene for a moment, then wound around Hugh's legs again.

Perhaps one of these mild, sunny days he would take Miss Herbert to view the lake. He was certain she would admire the swans. Everyone did. Pleased with the notion, he sauntered back into the house, the cat at his side, and along to his new picture gallery. He really needed to go to London to cast an eye over the selection on offer at the various art galleries to see what was for sale. He thought a nice landscape would look good over the mantel.

"Septimus, I need something as impressive as you."

The cat wore a smug look as though it agreed.

That he thought of Miss Herbert's reaction to such rather than Lady Susan's didn't occur to him at all.

Mrs. Herbert appeared less than satisfied with the account of Tabitha's day when told about it. "I confess it sounds dreadfully dreary, not to mention dusty."

Tabitha turned to her father. "When I am done, you must come to view the collection. I venture to say you will long to borrow several of the books I have seen so far. I have to resist the temptation to dip into a volume that catches my interest. His library is enormously varied."

Her father gave her a tolerant smile and agreed.

Tabitha studied her plate, pushing around the bit of chicken with sauce that remained. Dear Papa indulged her passion for reading, tolerating—but not really approving—it. Mama said nothing other than admonishing Tabitha to have good lighting when reading. Tabitha considered the baron. She could picture him in that large leather chair near the fireplace with light from a window pouring over his shoulder and the pleasant fire to toast his toes. What, she wondered, was his favorite reading? She was positive that books fascinated him quite as much as they did her. Else why would he have bought so many!

The remainder of the week passed in solitude. The baron had gone to London. Mrs. Dolman, the housekeeper, had informed her that he would likely return that weekend.

"Gone shopping, he said. Well, dear knows that he has the funds. But then, I fancy you know that." She sent a footman off with an empty crate.

Tabitha smiled, but made no comment. She was not one to gossip.

The housekeeper made a few more general remarks, reminded Tabitha when her nuncheon would be served, then went away leaving Tabitha to her work with Septimus for company. Tabitha chatted with the cat, but one-way conversations lacked a certain something.

At the conclusion of the week she gazed about with some satisfaction. All the crates had been emptied and were gone, leaving the incredible number of books stacked in neat piles around the perimeter of the vast room.

Crowder checked on her every day, his wispy brows rising as he saw all she accomplished. Now, the week ended, he ventured into the center of the room. "You still have a sizable amount of work to complete, Miss Herbert."

"Indeed," Tabitha agreed, "but I shall enjoy it."

A bustle in the central hall prompted Crowder to return to his business. Tabitha trailed behind him, suspecting that the baron had returned from his shopping expedition. She wondered what he had bought.

He stood, looking quite splendid in his many-caped driving coat and beaver hat, stripping off his York tan gloves. Tall, handsome, and rich—what an irresistible combination for any matchmaking mother. However, Tabitha thought she liked his dark brown eyes best of all.

Crowder gave instructions to two footmen regarding a parcel to be carried into the house while Tabitha hovered in the doorway to the entry hall.

The baron spotted her and beckoned her to join him. He wore a broad smile. "Come, I would have you see what I found. I had the most amazing piece of luck!"

Tabitha eagerly crossed the expanse of carpet to where the baron waited for his parcel to be brought inside, then followed as the footmen carefully carried it into the picture gallery. Obviously, it had to be a painting from the size and shape. She wondered what he had purchased.

"I went into this new gallery on the off chance I might find something of interest," he explained.

The painting was removed from its crate and gently leaned against the mantel at the baron's direction.

"It's done by a relatively new chap, John Constable. What do you think? I'm told it is of Flatford Lock and Mill." He stood poised before it, hands behind him as he gazed at his purchase with obvious pleasure.

"I've not been there but it is a charming picture. The sky is brilliant." She admired the rolling clouds that seemed so natural. "There is no artificiality to the scene, unlike so many painters who insert Gothic follies or Roman ruins into a pretty view. Their work seems affected, whereas this is so real, almost as

though you view the scene from a window or a pass-
ing coach."

The gilt frame became the work of art well, and
Tabitha thought it would look particularly well against
the walls hung with verdigris striped silk. "Over the
mantel, I fancy?" she inquired, believing that would
be best.

"Naturally." He nodded in agreement. "I am thinking of hiring the artist to come here to portray the
view of this house from across the lake. I rather fancy
that it would make a splendid painting."

"I have no doubt you are right. I confess I like this
realistic painting very much. Follies and ruins are all
very well in Italy, but hardly do here, do they?"

He nodded agreement. "We shall have tea, then I
will conduct you to the far side of the lake so you
might see what I mean about the view."

Tabitha shifted uneasily while indulging in a splendid tea complete with wafer-thin ginger biscuits and
seed cake.

Did the baron realize what he did by paying her
such attention? She doubted it. And she, heaven help
her, could not resist the time spent in his company.
He was the embodiment of her youthful daydreams,
the perfect dark-eyed hero. Alas, she didn't need res-
cuing from anything, save perhaps himself. She smiled
at the thought. Perhaps some of her romantic illusions
were crashing about her head?

Tea finished, she accepted his escort from the house.
They went out the door leading from the library to a
fine terrace with a view that she found enormously
pleasing.

"I sigh with delight every time I look out on this
view." She clutched the shawl draped about her
shoulders.

Hugh looked down at the glowing face turned up to his and smiled. He was not a smug man, but he knew that all he had worked to achieve in his garden had been accomplished. "It is rather nice, isn't it?"

"Nice is far too modest, my lord. It is a glorious prospect. I should very much like to stroll around the perimeter of the lake. Can it be done? I do not see a path." Her blue eyes had an engaging appeal in them as she peered up at his face. She was a bewitching little thing, so dainty and slender in her modest lilac muslin. He was glad to see the apron gone—it covered too much of her delectable form. The shawl only covered her slim shoulders.

"Actually, there isn't a path. That is no reason why we cannot have a pleasant ramble around it. In fact, with your clever mind, you may be able to give me an idea or two on how I could improve the view from here."

She shook her head. "I should think that impossible. But I would fancy a walk. Perhaps tomorrow? It is growing late," she said.

The sun was sinking toward the horizon, with soft gold tints washing the world below and gilding her face. "The morrow it is." He studied the girl near him. She looked quite lovely in the golden light. The sun accented her unusual silver gilt hair, richly tinting her skin.

"I shall look forward to it."

Since the following day was a Saturday, Tabitha had no qualms about abandoning her work in the library to take time for viewing the lake and the house from a distance.

He called for her in his shiny curricle, gratifying her mother no end. Papa came out from his study to exchange a few words about the progress made on the baron's books—or lack of it as the case may be, depending on one's view.

The baron said all that was proper and then they departed. They passed through the busy village on the way to his home. Rather than stop before the house, they drove around to the back. The baron halted and handed the reins to his groom.

Tabitha offered her hand to the baron, smiling in pleasure at his fine manners when he assisted her from the vehicle. A strange feeling deep within her at his company was ruthlessly suppressed. She had no business developing a tendre for him.

They went straight down from the house, then wound around the water's edge until at last they reached the far side. All the while they chatted amiably. She was amazed how he put her at ease. She was normally reticent when around gentlemen and he was quite impressive.

When they were opposite the house, he stopped. "Now, look. How do you think that artist might paint this view?"

"'Tis a superb vista, my lord! I think it will look very well in your picture gallery." She gazed first at the house, then the lake. Several white swans paddled about, offering a perfect touch of elegance to the view.

"Actually, I begin to think I should like it in the drawing room, above that fireplace. Have you seen it?"

"No, I have seen very little of your house." She wondered at his query. She couldn't see what possible credence he might give to her opinion. If Lady Susan Booth had an opinion, it would be different. Her young ladyship had decided views on almost everything from what Tabitha had observed.

He said nothing in reply. There was no earthly reason why she should be shown around his house. But she very much wished to see it.

They continued the stroll along the edge of the lake. She took a wary assessment of the large swans that neared. The baron seemed indifferent to their size and proximity, so she relaxed—slightly. But there was an old cob with a nasty glint in his eye she could not like.

"Those birds are not dangerous, are they?" She wasn't timid but these birds seemed very large to her eyes.

"No, I don't believe so. Why, I dare say that if you approach them, they would paddle away as fast as they could." He patted her hand where it rested on his arm, sending little tremors through her. She took a cautionary glance at him. He smiled down into her eyes, but it was almost avuncular, quite proper in fact.

His words were assuring, but Tabitha remained unconvinced, although she was far too polite to say so.

"I ordered the family portraits brought down from the attics and the rooms where they've hung to the picture gallery. Would you like to see what I have assembled?"

Tabitha nodded. In the back of her mind she wondered at the man she'd recently called the Black Baron. She now knew he was a quiet man, but most amiable on acquaintance.

Upon return to the carriage, they made the trip to the house in minutes. Perhaps he merely wished to see another's reaction to his paintings? That had to be it. She was certain of it. But his care of her rather impressed her.

Large oils ranged around the gallery, leaning against the verdigris silk at odd angles.

"You have a very well portrayed family," she observed after rotating to see all that were in the room.

"Vanity, I suppose. A good likeness was always to

be desired." He might have said more but a faintly heard disturbance in the entry hall captured his attention.

Crowder strode into the room, looking his most lofty. "Lady Susan Booth and her cousin Mr. Jasper West are here, my lord. Are you at home?"

"Of course. Show them in here." To Tabitha he added, "I will enjoy Lady Susan's comments. She is quite a witty lady. I've not met her cousin before."

Tabitha noted his frown, which immediately smoothed out as Crowder ushered the callers into the picture gallery. Lady Susan gazed about with obvious approval.

"Ah, so this is what Papa was telling me about! How grand! My lord, I am very impressed." She left her cousin's side to stroll over before the new Constable painting. "I heard you had gone to London," she gave him a twinkling look, "and fancy *this* is what you brought home."

"Well, let me have it—what is your verdict? I know you will not spare me." He sounded amused and tolerant of any opinions she might utter.

She spun about and pinned her older cousin with a look. "Jasper, tell me you recognize the artist." To Lord Latham she added in an aside, "Jasper is such a knowing one. He is *au courant* with simply everything in Town."

"Actually, I fancy I do know this chap. Constable, is it not?" He looked to Lord Latham for confirmation.

"Right the first time."

"Miss Herbert, what do you think? Oh, dear, I quite forgot to introduce you to Jasper. He is a cousin from my mother's side of the family—which is why he is not the heir!" She turned to study the other paintings. "Oh, very fine, my lord. All your notable relatives are here."

"Most are here. The others are confined to the drawing room. I think everyone in the family had a portrait done at one time or the other."

"Well, that is not so bad, is it? They are a handsome lot," she teased, her eyes flashing in an intimate smile.

"Miss Herbert has been assisting me with a project in my new library. Would you care to see it?"

"Indeed!" Lady Susan remarked to Tabitha, "I suppose you are one of those clever creatures who read worthy tomes and know ever so much. I never read. I believe it would give me the headache. Is that not so, Jasper?"

Tabitha listened as the cousins teased one another. Both had brown curls and dark eyes, only Mr. West's hair had been cut to make the most of his curls. She blushed when he caught her noting his dandyish appearance.

"You are assisting the baron?" He had a pleasant voice, although she had never been partial to tenors.

"Indeed, I am to catalog his new books."

"So you bought Ingoldby's library after all. Papa said it was devilishly expensive." Lady Susan chuckled.

Tabitha could see at once that the baron did not care for the reference to the cost. Naturally, he said nothing to that effect. How tolerant he was. Lady Susan was pretty and vivacious—he would forgive much from her. It was clear that those two would in all likelihood make a match of it.

"This is entirely wonderful, my lord," Lady Susan said with sparkling eyes and a wide smile once they entered the library. "My London Season was dull and dreary. It is good to be home again with dear friends."

Jasper West gave his cousin a sardonic look. "You are too hard to please, my dear girl. Turned down several proposals, although she won't talk about it."

"And that is proper, sir," Tabitha said, coming to

Lady Susan's defense. "Any girl who boasts about her conquests is not to be admired in my view."

Septimus crawled from behind a stack of books, drawing attention from the London come-out. "What a noble creature," Lady Susan cried. She strolled around the room, casting critical looks at the stacks of books. "How do you mean to arrange them, Miss Herbert?"

"I have yet to discuss that with Lord Latham. Either alphabetize by author, or have categories within which the books will be arranged."

"I think that once you are done, you must have a party to celebrate," Lady Susan insisted. She spun around, her pretty Norwich shawl swirling about her round gown of rich gold kerseymere. Her villager straw bonnet had matching gold ribands tied rakishly to one side of her face.

The baron gave Lady Susan an amused smile. "Why, if it is your pleasure, I shall. I suppose you want me to invite everyone from around here?"

"Naturally. At least, everyone who matters, that is. And you must be here, Miss Herbert, after having so much to do with the project." She sounded a trifle condescending.

Tabitha swallowed the ire that rose up. Her father might be a rector, but he was nephew to the Earl of Stanwell, and as such deserved a measure of respect.

"Then it is set?" Lady Susan's smile was self-assured.

The baron nodded. "When the last book is placed on its shelf, I promise I will have a party to celebrate."

"Good." Lady Susan beamed a smile of good will at Tabitha. "See that you hurry. I do so love a party."

Tabitha said nothing in reply, merely raising her brows. How could she possibly know how long it would take? She decided she was not going to be quick about it.

Chapter Three

Tabitha looked up from where she knelt on the library carpet when Lord Latham strolled into the room. "Good day, my lord. I am making satisfactory progress."

He had requested she arrange the books by topic, and within each topic sort them by the author's last name. She now dealt with the botanical section. "Do be careful, Lord Latham," she cautioned as he neared a stack of books.

He looked about, still not aware he was so close, and in the twinkling of an eye the books cascaded to the floor. He gazed at Tabitha with remorseful eyes. Then he grinned, that engaging look that so captured her heart. "I do apologize." He knelt to replace the books.

"Quite all right, believe me. I have been rather expecting it, given the number of piles around the room." She gave him a dry smile, forgiving him at once.

"Come and see what has come," the baron invited. He held out a hand, an imperative gesture she couldn't ignore.

She set aside the copy of *Curtis's Flower-Garden Displayed* to join him. Curious, she tossed her shawl over her shoulders and left her work to join him. This was an unexpected side of her employer, who was usually the most reticent of men. He seemed to have thawed of late. "Well?"

He merely shook his head, drawing her along with him.

She willingly walked beside him out of the front door and around to the side of the house, totally ignoring the delightful sensation created by placing her hand in his.

Here, in an utterly perfect spot, they came upon a man planting a fat shrub. Beside it on the ground sat a wire outline of a cat, crouching, as Septimus was wont to do.

"The *felis cattus couchant*!" Tabitha grinned, knowing he would recognize her reference to heraldic terminology.

"I suppose you think it ought to be *cattus rampant*? I doubt we could persuade Septimus to pose on his hind feet with forepaws battle-ready!" His look defied her to argue.

"I have done a lion like that, my lord." The gardener rose, dusted off his hands, and then arranged the wire cage over the plant. It required only a bit of trimming.

"Well, for the moment a cat is what we want." The baron stood admiring the potential topiary while Tabitha wondered how long it would take for the frame to be filled in completely so the cat would take green shape.

"By next year you should have a fine green cat."

"Can we wait that long, Miss Herbert?" The baron sounded serious, but a glance at his eyes revealed he teased. She didn't think he had ever teased her before.

"I should think you would not have much choice, my lord." Tabitha took a step away from him, conscious that by next year she would have little to do with the baron or his library, much less plants. "Plants will grow at their own predetermined speed. I daresay it will do well enough."

He made no reply. After murmuring a few words to the man, he escorted Tabitha back to the house. They entered the hall and here he stopped, capturing her hand.

"You said you had not seen the house. Come with me and I will show you a little of it."

She needed no urging to go with him. She had long desired to see the various rooms. In the drawing room she admired the Venetian window set into the east wall.

"I've heard of these, but yet to see one. Admirable, sir, admirable!" She pirouetted about to survey the room. The luscious red silk that hung on the walls was a perfect foil for the paintings displayed there. The drawing room was not only impressive, it looked surprisingly comfortable. It was a place where you could relax, yet entertain as well.

"I am pleased you like it. Look over here—above the fireplace. This is where I should like to have the painting of the house, if Constable will consent to do it."

"Excellent." Tabitha thought it highly unlikely that any artist would turn down a commission of such import.

They continued through the remaining rooms, Tabitha's head whirling with vibrant colors and exquisite furniture.

"Crowder said some furniture had arrived from London." She hesitated to ask what it was and where placed.

"I ordered a few things made from Chippendale's designs for the gallery. Would you like to see them?"

It took but a few minutes for them to enter that

room and Tabitha was struck silent at the pleasing arrangement of chairs. Papa had told her that most of the paintings here were the cream of Hugh's grandfather's collection, augmented by several fine paintings that the present baron acquired in recent years.

"I have not finished my collecting. I should like to fill all the rooms with choice art works." When she made a murmured reply he added, "These frames are made from Chippendale's designs. I like his taste, usually." The baron stood near her, hands behind his back while he examined a pair of Dutch genre scenes placed next to an ancestor.

Tabitha thought that had she an unlimited sum of money she would also furnish a room with such designs.

Everyone said the baron was to wed Lady Susan. The earl had frequently boasted he would be pleased at the union. Tabitha thought that he should wait to crow until the lady had been asked and she had accepted. Until then . . . anything might happen!

And she hoped it did.

The days were filled with her absorbing work. More often than not it seemed the baron required the use of his library desk, sitting there for hours at something or other. She liked his company, especially their discussions on books. She had not traveled, and thought his selection of travel journals and guidebooks fascinating.

"I should like to take a trip some day. Of course, that is not in my current plans, but I should like it all the same. Greece, I fancy. Perhaps Rome? And Switzerland if possible."

"Never give up hope for so worthy a prospect. I don't think we can ever guess what is in our future."

Tabitha could and did not want to face it.

*   *   *

The following Sunday Tabitha watched as Lady Susan and her cousin Mr. West entered the Earl of Montfort's enclosure at the front of the church opposite to where her family always sat. Lord Latham joined Lady Susan and her family. It would appear that the gossips were correct. It was only a matter of time before the betrothal would be announced. It was highly appropriate. Even Mama said so.

Tabitha stifled the strange yearning she had acquired while working with the baron in the library. There was little point in bemoaning what couldn't be changed.

Although Tabitha knew she ought to pay attention to Papa's homily, her attention drifted from his rolling periods to the pew box across the way. There was much to admire, from the modish bonnet Lady Susan wore to her vivid yellow pelisse trimmed with plum-colored ribands. Tabitha decided she would not have felt comfortable in such, yet on Lady Susan it looked quite perfect. Lord Latham seemed to admire it, at any rate. Tabitha approved his lordship in his excellent coat of fine blue wool over gray pantaloons. His garb seemed faultless in every way—like the man himself.

Tabitha studied her gloved hands, neatly folded in her lap. What had she expected, pray tell? It did her little good to daydream like the veriest romantic. So—following the service, she nodded politely to Lady Susan and her esteemed mother. She avoided Lord Latham's eye as well as that of Mr. West. Instead, she sought the company of a worthy young man—the squire's son, Sam Ainsworth. He was a staid gentleman, although his light gray eyes always had a friendly gleam in them when she was near. His straw-colored hair tended to go its own way, and his garb was that of a country gentleman. His boots had a decent gloss and his brown coat fit him for comfort, not high style.

Sam had been seeking her attention for months. Tabitha suspected he'd decided she would be a proper wife to him. It wasn't what she wanted, but how often does one gain one's heart's desire? She certainly didn't nurse a *tendre* for Sam Ainsworth!

"Miss Herbert." Lady Susan's voice reached Tabitha's ears from far too close to pretend she hadn't been heard.

"Lady Susan." Turning to greet her young ladyship, Tabitha curtsied properly.

"I teased Lord Latham into a date for his party," Lady Susan said. "A week from Saturday next, in the afternoon when the light will be best. His friends ought to be able to receive the invitation and respond by then."

"It depends on the distance." Tabitha suddenly recalled the presence of Mr. Ainsworth just behind her. She belatedly made the introduction.

"Mr. Ainsworth," Lady Susan trilled, "I trust you will join the party? If you are a friend of Miss Herbert you must attend." She smiled at Sam in her dazzling way.

"I would be pleased to come," he replied awkwardly. He took a step closer to Tabitha, looming over her like a protective hen with one chick.

Lord Latham joined them. He gave Sam a hooded look that could have meant anything. Tabitha had the notion that he wasn't pleased for some odd reason.

"By all means do join us. Miss Herbert, perhaps you will be so kind as to write out the invitations for me? I have noticed what a fine hand you have." While his words were polite, Tabitha saw a warm expression in his eyes.

She dropped her gaze to the pebbled path before the church. "I will be happy to oblige you, my lord."

"Good. Well, Lady Susan, we had all best be off."

Tabitha took a step back, bumping into Sam as she did. He steadied her with his hand. She hoped that Lord Latham would note that she was not alone. "Come, Mr. Ainsworth, we had best be on our way." Sam appeared only too ready to oblige her, guiding Tabitha along the path to the rectory.

Once she was safely distant from the earl's party, she bid Sam a civil good day and hurried into the house, feeling an utter coward. She could hardly deny that she would like to marry, but she intended to take her time. Better that, than to repent in the years to come.

"Tabitha, what had Lady Susan to say to you?" Mrs. Herbert interrogated her daughter at the dinner table.

"The baron is going to have a party to display the new picture gallery. She teased Lord Latham into having it."

Mrs. Herbert frowned. "Lady Susan is a trifle forward, it would seem. But I gather the alliance will take place."

"She is so lively and he is such a quiet gentleman. They scarce seem suited," Tabitha observed.

"You will learn that such considerations have little merit among marriages of the *ton*."

"I should think that similar tastes would strengthen a marriage. Lady Susan does not read, Mama."

"I daresay that in *her* case it does not matter." Mrs. Herbert exchanged a significant look with her daughter.

Come Monday Tabitha found the Latham house in turmoil. Mrs. Dolman bustled about charging the maids to this and that.

"Crowder, what is going on?" Tabitha inquired. It was yet two weeks until the party—or nearly so.

"His Lordship intends to have a friend or two come to visit, several relatives as well. Mrs. Dolman is busy."

"I see." Tabitha sped into the library. There, she found the baron at his desk. "Good morning, my lord."

"Ah, you are just the one person I want to see. Here is the paper we need for the invitations." He nodded at the nearby stack.

Tabitha quickly crossed to the desk. Beside the cream hot-pressed paper was a neat list of names. She was pleased to see her parents were on the list. Sam Ainsworth, too.

It did not take long for Tabitha to write and address the invitations. When she was finished she placed them neatly on the desk to await his frank.

"It is far too nice a day to remain cooped up in here. Let us go out to enjoy the view of the lake."

Not at all averse to enjoying his company, Tabitha eagerly left the house at his side, walking around to where the lake could be seen. She noted at once that a small rowboat was pulled up at the closest point. She didn't recall seeing it before. "You have a boat."

"I thought it might be agreeable to drift around the lake on a warm summer afternoon." He tucked her arm close to his side while they slowly strolled toward the lake.

"I daresay it would!"

"You like being out in a rowboat?"

"I don't know. I have not tried it before." Tabitha chuckled at his astonished expression.

"Not been in a little boat? That, we must rectify at once." In minutes they stood by the sturdy little craft.

Tabitha eyed it with misgivings. She didn't swim and heaven only knew how deep this lake might be. This, not to mention that wily old cob that lazily swam in circles out in the center of the lake, made her cautious.

Lord Latham urged her into the boat, setting her at the stern. Then he found the oars and put them into the locks. It took but a moment to place the anchor in the prow. He eased the boat from the shore, prepared to hop in.

They set off, enjoying the mild breeze and the scenery. Tabitha gave the swans a dubious look, especially the cob. It swam close to the boat, eyeing Tabitha with malevolence, as though it knew she couldn't swim.

"Go away." Tabitha made a shooing motion with her hands that gently rocked the boat.

The baron seemed amused. "He won't hurt you. The mute swans actually seem to like people. It isn't unusual for them to take food directly from a person's hand."

Tabitha glanced at him. If he thought she was going to try to feed those enormous birds he was out of his mind. "Somehow I find that bird rather intimidating." In a way Lord Latham affected her in like manner— he was a larger-than-life person who seemed to take her breath away far too often. "I have the oddest feeling that the bird dislikes me."

"Impossible. I cannot believe that a bird can take such a fancy." The look directed at her was the tolerant sort like any man gave a woman who had silly fancies. Tabitha noticed an older woman coming from the house. She waved a handkerchief at them, catching Lord Lathem's eye.

"I believe my aunt has come. We had best return to shore." He aimed the little boat in that direction at once.

Tabitha was quite pleased to be returned to land. It wasn't that she didn't trust his lordship to navigate safely on the water, she didn't trust that stupid bird.

Lord Latham brought the little boat to land, deftly handling the oars. He assisted Tabitha from the boat, then urged her up the slope to where they met his aunt. She had the look of the baron, somewhat. Her dark eyes and something about her manner proclaimed her a relative.

"What brings you here, dear Aunt? You can't have received my invitation yet," he queried, while drawing Tabitha to his side to make introductions.

"Wanted to see your additions. Always thought the house too small. Seems everyone is adding a library to his house these days. Introduce me to the young lady. She showed a lot of pluck to allow you to haul her about so."

Latham performed the introductions with the ease of one who has done it often. "Miss Herbert is assisting me with the books in the new library. We were taking a rest from tasks."

Tabitha curtsied as best she could given the slope of the lawn. "I am sure you will enjoy viewing all that the baron has done to his house." She was aware of his look of approval, seeming mingled with surprise that she would speak to his aunt in such manner. Well, she had been brought up to converse sensibly with strangers.

"Why do we not go inside? The wind is rising and I imagine Mrs. Dolman has tea waiting for us by now." The baron began to shepherd them to the front door.

The walk to the house was accompanied by the congenial conversation of the baron and his aunt. Tabitha listened with growing admiration. Somehow she hadn't pictured the baron possessing such a good relationship with his relatives. Not her Black Baron of years past. He had always seemed so removed, so aloof. Her imagination certainly had played her false. He was utterly charming.

They soon were inside where Crowder confirmed

the promise of a tea tray in the drawing room. They immediately sought the tasteful environs of that room.

"Well, I must say this is a nice introduction to your refashioned house. I trust you have something suitably impressive to follow?" Aunt Harriet accepted a cup of bracing tea, and then subsided on the red damask sofa, gazing around to take note of the changes that had occurred since she had last visited.

"I do my humble best, dear Aunt."

Crowder entered with a tray upon which reposed a generous selection of Miss Latham's favorite pastries and some little meat sandwiches the baron favored. Tabitha leaned forward in her chair to accept more tea when Crowder offered it.

It was then Septimus made himself known by insinuating his body directly in front of the butler in such a way that Crowder couldn't possibly have seen him. In a matter of seconds the butler stumbled, and tea splashed down the lower part of Tabitha's dress as he tipped the pot he offered. She hastily pulled her skirt away and jumped to her feet, for the tea had been very hot. She stared at the spectacle she made, a sopping dress held out before her while trying to maintain decorum. What a dreadful thing to happen!

The baron jumped up at once, setting his cup and plate aside while assuring Crowder it wasn't his fault. In the furor of the moment, the butler almost dropped the pot, inadvertently splashing some tea on the baron's breeches in the process. He jumped as the liquid spotted the fabric.

Hugh glanced at Miss Herbert, taking note that when she had to pull the gown away from her body, it revealed a trim, lithe form that captivated his senses. Fortunately his breeches, while damp, were not in as bad a state as her gown. He thought it likely it was ruined.

To Tabitha he said, "Go with the maid and she will see to it that your garments are washed and dried. I am certain that there must be a dress my sister left behind that will fit you." He looked to the maid, who nodded before leading Tabitha from the room.

"That is probably the prettiest assistant I have ever met, Latham." Aunt Harriet looked at him over the rim of her cup, her eyes dancing at his discomfiture.

Rather than reply to that leading remark, Hugh made his excuses, knowing full well that his aunt would continue her remarks when he returned from changing his clothing.

In his room he had a chance to reconsider the recent event that had so captured him. It was true he was more or less committed to Lady Susan. He admitted that. But he certainly found Miss Herbert intriguing. Lovely, too. How odd that he had been around her for weeks and not truly appreciated her exquisite form. Oh, he had noticed her hair, particularly when the sun brought out the silvery glints in the gold. But her form . . . ah, that was another matter entirely. She was delectable, quite perfect. Exquisite!

However, he knew what was expected of him. He'd tipped his hand by joining the earl in their enclosure last Sunday at church. It was only a matter of time before he was expected to propose to Lady Susan. He also knew, without conceit, that she would accept him. But for the first time he wondered if his intentions were wise.

When he left his rooms, he saw the maid he had assigned to care for Miss Herbert. "How is she?"

"Miss is changing out of her gown. I 'spect she'll be down before long." The maid bobbed a curtsy before hustling off toward the kitchens, carrying damp garments over her arms.

Hugh braced himself for his aunt's tart comments.

In the guestroom, Tabitha gazed with considerable awe at the gown she was to put on to replace her wet one. She slipped it over her head, then made a fruitless effort to do it up in the back.

How fortuitous that the baron's sister had left behind a gown of pale Nile green jaconet. It was slightly trained and surprisingly enough, it fit her. The neckline was too low, of course, but the sleeves were clever and reached her elbows, so perhaps that balanced. Besides, she doubted Lord Latham paid the slightest attention to what she wore.

The maid returned and quickly did up the dress. She also suggested she fix Tabitha's hair that had been tousled while in the boat. She drew it up on top of her head, allowing little curls to tumble down the back. Tabitha felt like another woman.

After thanking the maid, Tabitha made her way to the ground floor and along to the drawing room where she suspected Lord Latham would be entertaining his aunt.

"Thank you for the loan of a gown. I am all dry and prepared to return to my work." She paused by the door.

The baron turned about to stare at her, his mouth slightly open as though surprised.

Hugh stared at the vision standing near the door. He couldn't think what Grecian goddess she might be, but she must be one of them. She was a slender column of pale green with artless curls and a shy smile— a naiad, perhaps.

"My word!" Aunt Harriet exclaimed.

Chapter Four

Hugh stepped forward to better admire the beautiful young woman who entered the drawing room. It was Tabitha Herbert as he had never imagined she might be.

"Come, Miss Herbert, I think after all you have undergone that you should rest a bit. I can't think you would feel up to filing books now. Wouldn't you agree, Aunt Harriet?" He didn't bother to take his eyes off Tabitha. She made far better viewing than his aunt.

"By all means. You'd best have some tea," his aunt invited. "I always have found tea to be most restoring to my nerves." She gestured to the tea table before her.

Hugh glanced at his indomitable aunt. "I didn't know you possessed any, dear lady."

"Hmpf," she retorted. She turned her piercing gaze on Miss Herbert. "You enjoy your work, Miss Herbert?"

"Yes, indeed, ma'am." Tabitha's shy smile widened.

"I shall call you Tabitha." Aunt Harriet gestured to Tabitha to join her. White curls peeped from under a day cap edged with fine lace. Her eyes gleamed with curiosity.

"As you please, ma'am." Taking note of her effect

upon Lord Latham, Tabitha joined Aunt Harriet at once.

"She is a gazelle, Hugh. That is what her name means, and for once a woman actually lives up to her name." Her assessing gaze studied Tabitha with shrewd eyes.

Hugh thought his aunt was being more than usually outrageous, but in this instance he was compelled to agree with her. Tabitha did resemble a shy gazelle in a way.

Handed her cup of tea, Tabitha had little chance to truly enjoy it. Miss Latham fired one question after another at her. And rest was out of the question.

"So, what do you think of the books my nephew has acquired? Readable? Dull and dry?" She tilted her head and her eyes narrowed in expectation. "Well?"

"I say, Aunt, that isn't quite fair to put her on the spot like that." Hugh was curious as to what Miss Herbert might think, but he would never quiz her.

Her eyes flashed at him. "I think he has an interesting collection from what I have seen so far. I just shelved the novels and he has a good variety from *Evelina* to *Robinson Crusoe* and *Pamela*."

"*Pride and Prejudice* as well as that new book *Emma*, I fancy?" Aunt Harriet inquired archly.

"Why ma'am, he even has Charles Dibdin's book, *Hannah Hewitt or the Female Crusoe*—although that book came with the library he bought so we cannot blame him for that one."

"What else did you find of interest?" Aunt Harriet asked, a twinkle entering her hazel eyes.

"I confess I should like to travel and I spotted Mr. Eustace's book, *A Tour Through Italy* and Mariana Starke's, *Travels in Italy*. The Starke book looks most practical."

"And what sort of books do you have at home?"

Tabitha took a reviving sip of tea, then said dryly, "Papa gave me a copy of Fordyce's *Sermons to Young Women*."

"Worthy, indeed." Miss Latham murmured, fixing her attention on her teacup while avoiding her nephew's gaze.

Setting her teacup down on the tea table, Tabitha rose to excuse herself. "So much time has slipped past. I wish to arrange another stack of books." She looked to Lord Latham. "Before you know it, you won't have to worry about knocking them over. They will all be neatly shelved."

"There is something rather appealing about the smell of leather bound books." Miss Latham also rose from the sofa, an imposing woman in spite of her slim stature.

"Leather bound books, a hint of tobacco, and a dash of fine brandy go to create a perfect atmosphere," Baron Latham stated. "Comfortable chairs are not amiss, either."

"I think you ought to write a book, Latham. Maybe a history of the family or this area. Something on that order. I enjoy your letters," his aunt observed tartly.

"Merely because I can compose a decent letter does not mean that I can write an interesting book," he returned.

"Think on it."

Voices in the entry hall caught their attention.

"Dear Miss Latham," Lady Susan caroled as she wafted into the room. Golden ribbons danced about her hat as she made her way to the sofa to bestow a kiss on a powdered cheek.

"High spirits will do you in, my girl," Miss Latham scolded, giving Lady Susan a close look.

"Nonsense!" she replied with a dazzling smile.

Mr. West had followed his cousin into the room and stood quietly waiting off to one side.

Lady Susan spun about to wave at him. "My cousin, Jasper West. He's to spend the summer here."

"How nice," Miss Latham murmured.

Septimus wandered into the room, took one look at Lady Susan and hid behind the sofa.

"You frightened the cat, dreadful girl."

"Oh, pooh! But Latham dotes on that cat, so I had best mend my ways, I suppose?" She gave him a flirtatious smile that sent Tabitha to seek her work in the library.

"Do you find Susan overwhelming?" Mr. West inquired.

Surprised to see he had followed her, Tabitha held the book she had picked up before her as she turned to meet his gaze. "I wouldn't say that. I confess I do wonder . . . Lady Susan said she does not like to read. Not even novels?"

"If you mean *The Castle of Otranto* or something on that order, I fancy she might. I prefer *The Monk*."

"Well, I hardly thought she would enjoy a book like Brunton's *Self-Control*. That is so implausible." Tabitha gave him an amused look, then shelved the book she held.

He walked along the shelves, looking at the books that were there. "You have left a goodly amount of empty space."

"I fancy that Baron Latham or his descendents will wish to add to what is here. It would be tedious to be constantly rearranging, don't you think?"

Septimus strolled into the room, crossing to twine around Tabitha's legs, rubbing his head against her.

"Silly cat, I shall trip yet, between you and this

dress." She looked up at Mr. West to add, "After we went boating, we had tea and some was spilled on my dress. I had to borrow a gown."

"Susan said Latham contemplated getting a boat. Was it seaworthy?" He grinned. Suddenly Tabitha felt as though she was as charming as his cousin, Lady Susan.

"I fancy it is quite nice." She smiled. Maybe it was the borrowed gown. She'd noticed its effect on the baron.

"Having tea spilled on you must have been dreadful." His eyes held a lazy smile, predatory, actually.

She edged away.

"It was somewhat mortifying, actually." She scooped Septimus into her arms. He liked to have his chin scratched. She was glad to oblige, liking his rough purr.

"Funny about that animal. Most men don't care much for cats." Mr. West kept his distance from her and the cat.

"Septimus is unusual, I can quite see why Lord Latham is taken with him. He was the seventh of the litter, you see, and the seventh of anything is special."

"Village wisdom?" His voice mocked her.

Tabitha stepped away from him and tripped on her hem. He set her back on her feet, his smile rather mocking.

"Thank you." She was subdued for he was far too close.

"You are like quicksilver," he murmured in what she supposed to be a seductive manner.

"Isn't that a poison? I do not consider that very flattering, sir," she joked while edging away from him.

"You misconstrue what I meant."

"I think not. Perhaps I would just as soon not hear

words like that?" She thought he pretended to be offended.

"Well, so here you are!" Lady Susan breezed into the library and stopped short. "My, what an amazing number of books are shelved. You have been busy, Miss Herbert. Very busy, indeed." She advanced to where Tabitha stood in uneasy silence, still holding Septimus.

"The girl has intelligence, Lady Susan," Miss Latham stated firmly as she entered the library. "So rare nowadays to find a woman who actually reads something of value."

Lady Susan shrugged. "Few men place any importance on reading. I must say, my dear, that you do look ravishing in that gown. It reminds me of one of Elizabeth's. You needed dry clothes, of course, after the tea accident. Did your sister leave some things here?" she inquired of the baron, sidling up to him.

Tabitha's thanks were lost as the baron replied. "Miss Herbert was very gracious about the tea accident." He ignored the matter of his sister's dress.

"You could have been burned," Lady Susan cried.

Tabitha wished they would go away. "I jumped up right away so there was little chance of that."

"Yes, I saw it all," Miss Latham said. "Although, it was not Crowder's fault, you know. Septimus got in his way." She walked over to join Tabitha.

"True." Tabitha nodded, returning to her work.

"Why don't we go to inspect the new boat?" Lord Latham said coolly.

Miss Latham stayed with Tabitha while the others wandered off in the general direction of the lake.

"I do believe she intends to have him," Miss Latham mused aloud.

"Everyone says so," Tabitha replied.

"Everyone is not always right, you know." Miss Latham picked up Septimus and left the room to the
peaceful state that Tabitha preferred. Only, she found
it difficult. She was more convinced than ever that in
marrying Lady Susan the baron would be making a
huge mistake.

Several hours later when Tabitha was preparing to
leave Latham Court, Harriet Latham bustled into the
library looking around as though searching for
something.

"May I help you find whatever you seek?"

"Septimus. He was here and then he wasn't."

"I shouldn't worry. He likely has gone off to hunt
for a mouse or some such thing. He will return hungry
as a hunter, for he rarely catches anything." Tabitha
paused, trying to imagine the portly Septimus chasing
a mouse.

"Well, if you say so." Miss Latham was not
convinced.

"I wonder if my own dress is ready so I may change?
I cannot wear this home—I merely borrowed it."

"Knowing Elizabeth as I do, I imagine that she left
the dress behind because it was a mistake." Hearing
steps in the hall, she marched out to find the baron
approaching.

"Latham, tell this dear girl that when Elizabeth left
that gown here she hadn't the least notion of recovering it again. I just told Tabitha that she need not
change."

After a swift glance at his aunt, the baron nodded
in agreement. "Elizabeth orders gowns, thinking they
will do, then discovers they don't."

"Just as I said," Miss Latham confirmed.

"But I cannot, that is, this is such a lovely gown,
and I . . ." Tabitha floundered, not sure what to say.

"I shall have the maid fold up the dress you usually

wear for working for you to take with you. That gown becomes you far better than it did my sister!" The baron settled the matter, sending a maid for Tabitha's dress.

She expressed her appreciation. She traveled home in his coach as the weather had come on to rain. It was a treat to drive in such a well-sprung vehicle with beautifully cushioned seats, and fabric of the finest quality on the seats, doors, even the ceiling.

When her mother saw Tabitha in the gown she gasped. "Where did you come by such a fine creation?"

"Lord Latham said his sister Elizabeth had left it behind. It seems she often makes mistakes and this was one of them. I must say, for a mistake, it is quite pleasing."

"It's a blessing her husband can afford mistakes!"

Then Tabitha related the happenings of the day.

"Best say nothing of your tea accident and need to change your dress. Who knows what your father would say."

"I shall be as mute as a fish, Mama."

The next morning brought Tabitha to Latham Court. In the library she found Miss Latham prowling around.

"Dear ma'am, is there a problem?"

"Septimus did not come home last night."

"How dreadful. He never misses a meal from what Lord Latham says." At an amused look from the lady, Tabitha added, "You must admit, that cat is decidedly plump."

"Decidedly. I have looked everywhere. Although Latham has not said much, I know he is concerned. I heard him asking Jamison about it earlier and the bailiff hadn't seen the cat either. I miss that animal."

"Where have you *not* searched?"

"I have hunted from top to bottom in this house—well perhaps not the attic, but the cat would never go up there. Nor the basement, either." She turned to face her nephew.

"I agree. I asked Jamison to check around. All we can do is wait." He shoved his hands in his pockets and paced back and forth before the tall library windows.

"Could he have wandered into a room accidentally, then had a door shut on him by error?" Tabitha imagined there were any number of little closets in the house.

"Why have we not heard him?" Miss Latham asked. "He is able to give voice to his displeasure when he wants."

"Well, I shall go about my duties for now," Tabitha said politely. She was not paid to hunt for a cat. She worked steadily until noon. Miss Latham came to scold her.

"It is dreadful of you to be so industrious. I must say Latham is too hard on you!" she said indignantly.

"Is it time for a nuncheon, dear ma'am? The hours slip by far too quickly." Tabitha joined the older lady in a walk to the dining room.

"That animal has not returned." Miss Latham snapped her words. Tabitha could tell how distressed she was.

"Would you like me to investigate? Perhaps a stranger can think of a place you have overlooked?"

They ate sparingly, both preoccupied. When done, they returned to the central hall just as Crowder opened the door to permit Lady Susan and Mr. Jasper West to enter.

"Such gloomy faces!" Lady Susan exclaimed.

"Is something amiss?" Mr. West inquired.

"Septimus has gone missing. We have not seen the cat since sometime yesterday. Hugh is that upset."

"Over a mere cat?" Lady Susan said with a laugh.

"Susan is a dab hand at finding things." Mr. West gazed down at his cousin. "Why don't you try?"

She gave him a rather odd, somewhat mystified look. "I shouldn't know where to begin."

Thinking of all the little rooms that must be below-stairs, Tabitha murmured an excuse to Miss Latham, then headed for the lower regions of the house.

Here were storage rooms, the various offices. She opened doors to each, but found no cat. Her instinct leading her on, she crossed through the main part of the basement to the area below the picture gallery.

"Septimus? Where are you?"

She was rewarded with a faint meow. Door after door was opened until at the very last one, a furry body flew out to virtually attack her, twining about Tabitha's legs in a frenzy of annoyance.

"Yes, yes, I know you are displeased. But I have you now and we shall find something delicious to restore you."

Deciding it was best to feed the cat before bringing it upstairs, she did just that. Once Septimus satisfied his hunger and thirst, they went up the narrow stairs until reaching the inner hall. She could hear Miss Latham fretting to Lady Susan, with Mr. West urging her young ladyship to exert her powers of detection and Lady Susan demurring.

"Never mind. I have the cat." Tabitha went around the corner into the central hall. "Mrs. Dolman said no one has been in those storage rooms in days, so who knows how Septimus got there." She placed the animal on the floor.

Septimus took one look at Mr. West and hissed, back up and tail in a fluff. His eyes narrowed in green fury.

"How strange, Mr. West. It would seem that the cat does not like you." Aunt Harriet turned to greet her nephew with the news. "Tabitha found Septimus. Where was he?" Aunt Harriet scooped up the cat to offer him to Lord Latham.

"Dashed odd how you can become attached to a pet," Latham said. "He irritates me at times, but when he isn't around I miss him. You found him?" The cat settled down in his master's arms and stared out at Mr. West and Lady Susan with the haughtiest expression imaginable.

"In that last storeroom below the picture gallery. Mrs. Dolman said no one has been there for days. Poor Septimus could have starved to death." Tabitha didn't think the cat had managed to go in there by himself.

"Well, he is only a cat, after all," Lady Susan said with a charming smile and a half-laugh.

Mr. West nudged her, although Tabitha suspected she was the only one who observed it. "What you mean to say, dear cousin, is that while it is a cat, it is a very special cat. Do I not have the right of it?"

"Oh, of course." Lady Susan beamed a sugary smile.

Tabitha wondered how sincere Lady Susan was, although she perhaps was not fond of cats and therefore didn't understand how attached one could get with a pet. She noted that Lady Susan kept her distance from the animal.

"We came over to offer our help in planning your party to show off the picture gallery. We had no idea there was a crisis here. Isn't that so, Jasper?" Lady Susan said.

"How kind of you," Lord Latham began when the sound of a coach arriving at the front of the house was heard.

Crowder opened the front door and made his stately progress to the coach.

"I recognize that vehicle," the baron murmured to his aunt. "If that isn't Elizabeth I shall eat my hat."

"Cat? Oh, dearest, you mustn't do that!"

"Hat, Aunt, not cat." He hastened to the door, putting the cat down at once.

"Well, well. Elizabeth! And to what do we owe the pleasure of your company?"

"I was bored. And I wished to see your new library and picture gallery. I want dear Purcell to do the same."

The young woman hurried to give her brother a kiss on his cheek. She had light brown hair and the same hazel eyes her aunt possessed. "Dear Aunt Harriet! How lovely to see you! Oh, I have been clever to come now. I can see that! We shall have a delightful time." Her restless gaze moved to Lady Susan and Mr. West. "Lady Susan, how nice to see you again." She gave the gentleman a look of inquiry.

"My cousin, Jasper West, who is spending the summer with us." Lady Susan gave him an ardent glance.

"How very pleasant for you, my dear." Then her gaze fell upon Tabitha, standing off to one side.

"Latham, introduce me to this charming young lady."

"Miss Tabitha Herbert, daughter of our rector. She is kindly helping me catalogue the library of books I bought."

"How smart of you—to find someone who not only can do your books but is good to look upon." Elizabeth beamed at Tabitha with a sweet expression.

A tall well-built gentleman entered the hall, coming

to stand by Elizabeth. She gave him an adoring look that spoke well for their marriage.

"Purcell! Good to see you. Miss Herbert, this handsome chap is my brother-in-law, George, Lord Purcell." The baron introduced the others, then led them into the drawing room.

Tabitha would have returned to the library, only Miss Latham took her firmly by the arm and brought her along. "I wish you to become acquainted with my niece. I believe the two of you will get along famously. Elizabeth and Lady Susan do not agree. Having you with us will undoubtedly ease matters." She gave Tabitha a wicked little smile.

Tabitha could not imagine how this might be. It was difficult to deny Miss Latham, however. She might be a sweet old lady—she was also a force of nature.

At the doorway, Miss Latham paused to inquire in a low voice, "Tell me again where you found Septimus."

Tabitha repeated her story, then added, "It is my considered opinion, ma'am, that there was no way the cat could have gone in that room on its own. Since the room was but rarely accessed, I believe that someone had to put him there! But *who* would have done such a thing?"

Aunt Harriet gave Lady Susan's cousin a speculative look. "Why do I have the feeling Mr. West may have had something to do with it? The cat gave him a ferocious glare." She exchanged a look with Tabitha that said volumes.

Chapter Five

The day after the Purcells arrived was filled with discussions how best to entertain the expected guests for the gallery and library exhibition—such as it was.

Elizabeth kept asking Tabitha's opinion, sending little twinkling smiles at her until she felt flustered.

"I fail to see why you do not contribute your sensible ideas." Elizabeth's hazel eyes were full of mischief. "Unlike some others around here, you have such a practical mind. We can use precisely such at this moment."

"Oh, how can you say such a thing?" Tabitha scolded. "My family would not agree with you at all!" Her sisters believed her to be a romantic, given her love for Gothic novels. No, she was not a practical girl. If she were, she would not have tumbled for the darkly handsome baron.

Tabitha had worked diligently at shelving the books, and thought she made excellent headway. She wanted nothing more than to complete the work she had been hired to do and leave the man who had captured her foolish heart.

When one of the younger maids offered to assist, Tabitha made use of her, jotting down the pertinent information on the various books before directing the girl where to place them. It speeded up the work considerably.

Lady Susan and her cousin Jasper were at Latham Court far more than Tabitha expected; however, given her suspicions regarding the young lady, it didn't surprise her in the least. Lady Susan wasn't interested in charming the baron's sister. She was intent on snaring the baron. Tabitha thought that she was making considerable progress.

Tabitha made a point of chatting with Sam Ainsworth on Sunday as the party from Latham Court passed them when leaving church. She waved gaily and tried to look happy.

Sam might be a ruggedly pleasant-looking man, but he had no use for books, preferring hunting, shooting, and dogs. There would never be a book room in his house. As far as she could recall, the closest thing was the small office where records were kept and the documents pertaining to his horses and dogs were located—plus a few studbooks.

"Come let us see who has answered the invitations to the grand viewing." Aunt Harriet bustled into the library with her list, locating at once the list of those invited.

Tabitha set aside the books. She paused while she checked the list, eyeing the dear lady hesitantly. "Lady Susan invited Mr. Ainsworth after church. He *is* the squire's son and a prominent person in the area. And . . . a friend of mine." That was putting it delicately enough.

"So I see," Miss Latham agreed with seeming reluctance, giving Tabitha a reproving look.

"Are we to wish you happy, Miss Herbert?" Lord Latham inquired, an inscrutable look on his face.

To such a nonsensical query Tabitha demurely remained silent, thankful for once that she blushed. She had often found that silence was a sensible refuge when she didn't want to reply. Words had a way of coming back to haunt her.

She dreaded the party, even if it would likely be the event of the season. Probably the betrothal would be announced then, for it was the perfect occasion. Everyone would be there and what better time to announce that Lord Latham intended to marry Lady Susan?

Tabitha revealed the party plans to her mother, who marveled at the lavishness. That the Herberts had been included satisfied Mrs. Herbert no end, while the reverend appeared to take it as his due.

Several days following the announcement of the party guest list, the baron wandered into the library to take note of the progress that had been made.

Since his sister and her husband had arrived, he had found little time to work at his desk. Tabitha had missed their conversations. He was not only widely read, but also widely traveled. She admitted that she worked faster when alone. He was an attractive distraction, one she had best dismiss.

"You are almost finished! I cannot believe the amount you have accomplished this week." He looked down at the remaining stacks, touching one stack with the toe of his finely polished boot.

"I have had a bit of help." She knelt on the floor. "I can place any remaining books on these lower shelves during the party. Also, there are cupboards in the next room where books can be stored. Someone placed a number of old books there at some point in the past."

"Are there, indeed? Well, by all means do as you please about them." He frowned, turning to look at the door. "That's odd, I don't recall any books in there."

"They look rather old and a trifle tattered. We can

look at them now if you like." She rose to her feet
in preparation to fetching the old books should he
want them.

He shook his head at this notion. He had something
else on his mind. "You seem to be on rather good
terms with the younger Mr. Ainsworth. When I see
you after church you are busy flirting." He sounded
put out. "Your local beau?"

Refusing to explain what she thought of good old
Sam, Tabitha merely gave his lordship what she hoped
was an enigmatic smile. She temporized, "He is a good
member of the church. I try to talk to as many people
as I can."

"He hovers over you like a vulture," he muttered.

"Oh, surely not a vulture! Say, a suitor, rather."
Tabitha didn't know why she felt it necessary to trot
out Sam as a beau, but it soothed her pride a bit. The
man she loved was intending to marry another woman
and she didn't wish him to think *she* was totally on
the shelf.

Hugh left the library displeased with everything. It
looked to him as though Mr. Ainsworth was well on
his way to claiming Tabitha Herbert. His attentions
were marked, and she seemed accepting of them. He
had no right to complain, although he wished he
might. Yet what would that accomplish? His path was
set, his duty fixed.

Upon entering the entry hall he found Lady Susan
and her cousin being shown in by the dignified and—
to Hugh's eye—disapproving Crowder.

Without waiting for Crowder to say a word, Lady
Susan glided across the hall to greet Hugh with a
broad smile. She wore yellow and bloomed with good
health. Hugh supposed he could do worse than marry
the lovely daughter of his neighbor. That he didn't

love her made little difference. His sister married for love, but he suspected that few actually did.

"You planned all the details. I *so* wanted to assist you!" Susan pouted, tucking her hand around his arm.

He disliked clinging women. However, one forgave beautiful women much—and Lady Susan was all of that.

"So we did. What else ought we have besides food?"

"Music! You really ought to have some music. If you put the musicians in this hall, you could have dancing. Otherwise, it would be dreadfully dull. Once the guests inspect your pictures and cast a look at the library what is there for them to do—but gossip? *That* is dull."

"Heaven forfend we should have a dull party. We shall enjoy good food, however." He smiled at her nonsense.

"You always serve delicious dishes. I had no thought it would be otherwise. The offerings will be appetizing as usual. No, we need entertainment—music."

"Do you have any thoughts on the matter, Mr. West?"

"Call him Jasper. After all, we are neighbors and bound to see much of one another." She giggled softly.

Her wiles failed to entice him. It was a pity he was drawn to Tabitha Herbert, who was likely going to marry the squire's son. Hugh was of a mind to marry, and if he couldn't have the one he wanted, he might as well marry a woman who obviously wanted him. And as her father wished.

They strolled into the library, chatting about the music, speculating on the number of people who would accept, and leaving Jasper West behind.

"Lady Susan . . ." the baron began in an intimate manner.

Tabitha rose from where she had been kneeling. "Excuse me." She whisked herself from the library in a trice. She had a premonition of what was about to transpire and she wanted to be gone. She ran into Elizabeth in the entry.

"You look flustered. Where is my brother?"

Tabitha cast a glance back at the library and shrugged. "I left him in the library with Lady Susan."

Elizabeth flashed Tabitha a look of dismay. "Has he, that is, did he? Oh, dear." She took Tabitha by the arm, leading her through to the drawing room, requesting that Crowder bring a tray with tea and biscuits.

"I would not be the least surprised if there will be a betrothal to celebrate at this coming party." Tabitha stared out across the lawns and shrubbery. She had no wish to meet Elizabeth's eyes for fear that her true feelings might be revealed to one so astute.

"You think so? Well, it is not what I had hoped for, but I daresay everyone else expects it. Goodness knows her father has been dropping hints forever. It would be sensible, I suppose. Our land marches with the earl's and Lady Susan inherits everything." She paused a moment before adding, "It is unlike him to bungle something so important. Hugh usually does so well." She urged Tabitha to the sofa.

Tabitha thought it prudent not to respond to words that were little better than audible musings.

The muted red upholstery of the chairs and sofa was reflected in the delicate Moorfields carpets on the oak floor. It was a comfortable spot for a chat. The tray with the tea and biscuits was brought. The tea proved to be just the thing to revive Tabitha's flagging spirits.

"I wonder what . . ." Elizabeth cast a doubtful look in the vague direction of the library.

Not misunderstanding her in the least, Tabitha calmly replied, "I expect we shall know sooner or later. Would you mind if I went home now?" She had no excuse. She did not feel ill—at least in health. Her heart ached, but a girl didn't actually become ill or die from heartache, did she?

"Of course. I will make your excuses to Aunt Harriet, and to Hugh should he inquire. He has been abstracted of late. Perhaps we know the reason why now?"

"Perhaps." How did a lovelorn man behave? If he was. Lovelorn, that is. She wondered.

Not wishing to return to the library for her white apron, Tabitha hastily left the house in a flurry of skirts for the stables. Once there, it was but a brief time before the gig was ready and she could flee Latham Court.

Her mother was clearly surprised when Tabitha returned so early in the day. "Is anything amiss?"

"There are things afoot at the Court. If I make no mistake, Lord Latham and Lady Susan will be announcing their betrothal at the coming party."

"I see," Mrs. Herbert murmured after a swift look at her daughter's face. "It is not unexpected, love."

During the following days Tabitha made it a point to keep out of everyone's sight and way as much as possible. At last Lady Harriet sought her out.

"You *are* coming to the party? Your parents as well? And Mr. Ainsworth, I suppose?" Miss Latham plumped herself down on one of the cozy leather chairs before the library fireplace. "And you will wear that Nile green gown? By the by, Elizabeth had completely forgotten it until I asked."

"If you believe it proper, I shall. It is far finer than anything I own. I confess I like it very much."

Miss Latham appeared to mull over something a

few moments, then said, "You fair flummoxed my nephew when you first wore it. I should like to see its effect again."

"He is to marry Lady Susan. While they haven't announced it, everyone knows."

"He does not have the air of a happily betrothed man. He looks more like someone who has agreed to a contract that might benefit him. I should think he could do better than that!" She sounded highly indignant.

Tabitha knew better than to comment.

"She has no love for him—or anyone else unless I am greatly wrong. She has affection for her cousin Jasper from all I have observed. Odd, that."

"True." Tabitha cast a puzzled look at Miss Latham. "Indeed, they are very attached. I have seen that with other cousins, however. It is not so unusual."

"If you say so." She frowned. "I trust Mrs. Dolman will have things in hand come Saturday."

"You know she will, ma'am. Cease your fretting. Look on the bright side. Your nephew has found a girl to marry and we should all be pleased, for there will soon be an heir for Latham Court and all its treasures and fortune."

Miss Latham merely sniffed, then left the room.

Saturday afternoon Tabitha was not in any great rush to leave the rectory for Latham Court. She dawdled until her mother sharply reprimanded her. "*You* may have seen it all, but *we* have yet the pleasure of viewing it. Come!"

The avenue leading up to the Court revealed that many carriages had arrived. The coachman stopped before the front entrance. Within minutes the steps had been let down. Tabitha and her parents approached the house to be let in by a dignified Crowder.

"It is good to see you, Miss Herbert," he said after directing her parents into the new gallery.

"How have things been here, Crowder?" He might be dignified, but he was also a dear man.

"Tolerable. You have been missed around here, and that's no mistake. Even the cat seems to look for you."

"How kind you are to make me feel so wanted. I expect I had better find Lady Purcell. She expressly said she wished to see me in this gown." Giving Crowder a mischievous look, she glided away to search the assemblage for Elizabeth. Her husband was seen at once, his height making him easy to spot. Elizabeth stood at his side. Tabitha thought she looked bored to her toes.

"Tabitha! How glad I am to see you! Come with me at once. You must show me something in the library."

Following willingly in her impetuous path, Tabitha wondered what was on Elizabeth's mind. "Well?" she said, once they were in relative peace.

"We had the right of it. You missed the announcement. The earl simply could not wait to blurt out the impending marriage between his only child and the rich baron."

"Heavens! He didn't put it like that, surely?"

"No, but he might as well have done," she grumbled.

Tabitha turned her head to stare blankly at a shelf of books. How stupid she was! She had known this was coming.

"I must say, that dress is enormously fetching on you. It made me look as though I was about to succumb to a bout of jaundice." She led Tabitha back to the central hall where she paused, looking about as though searching for someone. "Hugh's friend, Sir Anthony Fleming, is here. I know you will captivate him! He is quite dashing and you, my dear girl, outshine even Lady Susan this afternoon. She looks jubilant, as though she has won a prize. Which she has, I must say, for Hugh is the dearest man. I fancy I am biased, but I think he deserves better. You, my dear Tabby, are a delicious conserve upon which to feast the eyes." She tugged at Tabitha's hand, drawing her through the crowd to where a tall blond fellow stood chatting.

"Tabby?" Tabitha inquired, surprised at a pet name.

"Septimus likes you and I think you are as cozy a friend as he is." Elizabeth winked, smiling at her friend.

All of which made not the slightest sense to Tabitha. Her speculation ended when they arrived before the stranger. He bowed to Elizabeth before eyeing Tabitha.

"Sir Anthony, a woman after your own heart—she enjoys books. In fact, she is the one who has catalogued Hugh's."

A slow smile creased his good-looking face. "This is truly a pleasure, Miss Herbert. Hugh mentioned you more than once. Come, you must show me what you accomplished."

Tabitha walked with Sir Anthony to the library where she gestured to the walls of books. "As you can see, he has acquired a considerable number of books. I've had the pleasure of cataloging them. It's not been a dull task. My brother calls me a bookworm—although not exactly blue."

"You mean you read something other than 'improving' books, I gather?" He grinned down at her, looking utterly charming and incredibly dashing in his gray coat and dove gray pantaloons with a green waistcoat on his trim form.

Tabitha smiled—demurely, she hoped. "The baron has brought in some furniture now I'm about finished. Those library steps over there, a reading table, comfortable chairs, and this handsome piece to house large books."

"I see the painting of his parents hangs over the fireplace. They were a fine couple. Pity they had to die so young." He studied the picture a few moments before turning away to survey the room. "He has done himself proud with these additions."

"True. I couldn't imagine anything finer," she said.

"It would be an excellent place on an inclement day. What have you remaining to do in here?"

"The oversize books, of which there are perhaps two dozen. Some books on music and musicians. Not much beyond that." She eyed the leather strip that protected a shelf.

"I suspect Hugh has welcomed your company. I wish I knew what prompted this betrothal to Lady Susan. Was it of long standing, this connection?" He frowned fiercely at a framed collection of butterflies of the countryside.

"I believe Lord Latham's late father and the earl hoped the pair would wed. It was long expected." Tabitha did not say that there were those who had nurtured other hopes. How silly of Elizabeth to consider . . . what?

The delicate sound of music drifted into the room, an indication that people seemed to have had their fill of viewing the pictures as well as the library and books.

"Ah, music. Will there be dancing?" he queried.

"I believe there is to be music while we enjoy a

buffet repast in the dining room. After that, there may be dancing." Tabitha wished she might disappear. She wouldn't miss the gentleman at her side. He was nice-looking, and certainly not poor, given his appearance. But . . .

"La! There you are!" Lady Susan whisked into the room, her gown of yellow sarsenet floating about her slim form. "Sir Anthony, you have one of our luminaries. Hugh would still be searching for a librarian were it not for Miss Herbert's kindness in coming to his aid." She waved her hand about and Tabitha steeled herself not to show any reaction when she spotted the simple sapphire ring.

Tabitha wished she might dislike Lady Susan, but with the best will in the world she could not. True, she yearned for another gentleman to lure Lady Susan to his arms, leaving Lord Latham free. But then, that would do no good, for Tabitha had little expectation that she would take Lady Susan's place as the future Lady Latham.

"I am well aware I have a treasure in Miss Herbert."

Lady Susan laughed gaily, her eyes sparkling. "Come, Sir Anthony, for I wish to dance with you. You'll release him, Tabitha?" She beamed a smile on Tabitha, her delight in her betrothal party evident.

"I have no claim on the gentleman. He is yours if you wish it." Tabitha watched the two depart, before wandering over to gaze out of one of the tall, beautifully draped windows. There was an exquisite garden to be seen from this end of the house. One window stood ajar and a slight breeze scented with early summer flowers entered the room.

"If we stepped out there, we could be in the garden. Let's explore a bit." Lord Latham now stood by her side.

"Sir," Tabitha protested. "You would not neglect

your guests or your newly betrothed Lady Susan!"
Her heart galloped madly.

"They are all either busy eating, gossiping, or—like
Lady Susan—dancing. I deserve a bit of peace."

She placed her hand confidingly in his, liking the
strength, the warmth she found. He drew her like a
lodestone. There was something innately good, yet de-
liciously tempting about Hugh Latham. He might be
Baron Latham, but scarcely the Black Baron she
once thought.

They were on a narrow terrace, close to the garden
where flowers began to bloom. Off to one side Septimus sat in lordly splendor on a bench, surveying the
world with a supercilious eye. He blinked at them.

"I have seen little of you today. You are enjoying
yourself?" He released her hand at her slight tug.

"Indeed, who could not? Everyone has remarked
on the excellence of your additions. Even your selection of books has met with general approval."

"You have not said how *you* feel." He turned to
face her. "Surely you need not hide your feelings from
me. Should we have left off the music?"

"Oh, no! Lady Susan enjoys dancing. I do as well."
The strains of the music, a waltz—no doubt played
at Susan's request—drifted through the open window.

"Dance with me," he commanded gently.

"I do not think that wise, sir." She gazed up at him
wondering if the longing she felt showed in her face.

"That is all the more reason to be my partner."

She yielded, for she truly did wish to swirl about in
his arms. Such is the stuff that spinsters clutch to their
bosoms. It was far better than her hopes and
expectations.

"Miss Herbert . . . Tabitha . . . I shall miss you.
Promise me you will not be a stranger to me . . .
to us."

"I make no promises, my lord. I may travel. I mean to visit my sisters," she improvised. "I shall go about the country from one to another for as long as I am able." She forgot that she had given the impression she was to be engaged to Sam Ainsworth.

Hugh gazed down at the lovely woman in his arms and knew he had made a terrible mistake. It was not Lady Susan he wished to wed. It was Tabitha Herbert. And . . . she was on the verge of wedding the squire's son.

What a frightful tangle!

Chapter Six

Lord Latham bowed politely as she stepped away at the conclusion of their dance. "It has been my pleasure, Miss Herbert." His handsome face was a polite mask although his dark eyes appeared to have a warmth in them she had not seen before. She had no clue as to what he might be thinking. But he had been slow to release her hand when the music ceased, a thing she would long treasure.

She curtsied, murmuring something in reply before excusing herself to find her parents. Surely she had spent enough time at the affair that she might leave? The waltz with the baron had been a mistake. It had made her yearn for another. She made for the entry hall and her parents.

Sir Anthony joined her, spiriting her off to the gallery with droll comments on one of the paintings. His funny comments had her laughter echoing in the entry hall.

Hugh followed them, taking note just how Tony had appropriated her. Why had he invited that smooth fellow? True, he was a good friend, but Hugh wondered if he might not be persuaded to attract Lady Susan rather than Tabitha.

The only way out of his dilemma was for Susan to

change her mind. And that lovely charmer had been led to think Hugh was hers. He was an honorable man and should honor his offer of marriage, but now he wished otherwise.

Hugh hadn't missed the slip Tabitha had made. There had been nothing said about a marriage to Sam Ainsworth. It sounded like she planned to be a spinster aunt. If she had paid the slightest attention to Mr. Ainsworth this evening it had been when Hugh wasn't around, he thought smugly. She couldn't be enamored of that clodpole!

She had worn that Nile green dress again. It looked stunning on her, with her silver gilt hair swept up on the top of her head. There were no ribands or fa-lals for embellishment, just her pretty curls. No necklace at her slender throat, either. He noticed that she had the creamiest of skin that looked soft as the finest satin. It was small wonder that Tony was captivated with her.

Hugh hadn't the slightest notion if Tabitha Herbert cared for him. He desired to know if the intelligent, charming Tabitha would welcome his attention once he was free. Butterfly-like Susan should easily find another man.

He would have a talk with Tony later. The best of friends, surely he might be counted upon to help?

Tabitha had to laugh at the remarks Sir Anthony made about one of the older portraits. True, the face looked as though the sitter had been eating lemons before the artist painted her likeness. "We are not kind, sir."

"Well, she has been dead these many years, so I doubt she will mind." He paused, then continued, "Will you be here on Monday to resume your work?"

"I believe so. Why?"

"Ah, I shall remain in that event. Hugh invited me to stay on and so I shall." His smile was rather smug.

"Lord and Lady Purcell will be here as well as Miss Latham. You will have excellent company."

"Elizabeth is a great gun and George is a good fellow. Aunt Harriet is a dear." He slowly strolled along the length of the room with her, admiring the paintings.

"True. Have you known the family very long?"

"Hugh and I went to Eton and Oxford together. That creates a bond of some standing. He is a jolly good chap, none better. I feel sure you have found him tolerable?"

"In respect to the library? Yes. He has been all that is amiable." Too amiable as far as she was concerned. He was so amiable that she had tumbled into love with him.

"Tabitha? Oh, there you are," Mrs. Herbert said as she bustled around the corner. "Your father wishes to depart."

Tabitha made her excuses, not truly sorry to leave the charming Sir Anthony.

She wondered when her regard for Hugh had altered into love. Only she mustn't think of him as Hugh, always Lord Latham. But Hugh was a good name, solid and respectable. His betrothal was a mistake. Lady Susan needed someone more like herself. Jasper West was far more suited to her vivacious temperament. And she never read books—except a Gothic novel. It didn't bode well for Hugh's future happiness if his wife couldn't share his interests.

The Herberts made their adieus, and were driven home in the luxurious barouche that had brought them.

"Lord Latham is amazingly thoughtful, is he not,

Tabitha?" Mrs. Herbert trailed a finger along the rich velvet of the seats. "Fancy his having this gorgeous carriage waiting for us. He's different than I'd believed."

"He has been very kind to me," Tabitha allowed.

"And why should he not, pray tell," Mr. Herbert inquired. "As our daughter you merit every consideration."

Tabitha smiled fondly at her parent. If he thought that being a Herbert could begin to compare with being the daughter of an earl, he was not accepting reality.

Sunday brought the morning service where—as usual—Tabitha sat on her side of the aisle, while the group from Latham Court sat across. Lady Susan sat between Lord Latham and Sir Anthony. Mr. West looked irked.

It was after church when she saw Lady Susan clinging to Lord Latham's strong arm, beaming up into his face with all her charm, that Tabitha hatched her idea. Could she do it? Another look and she determined that she must.

So, when Sam Ainsworth joined her, she clung to his arm and copied the flirtatious smile that Lady Susan wore. "Good day, Mr. Ainsworth." She batted her lashes, choking back laughter at his expression. He was clearly taken aback. He preened a trifle because she was the rector's daughter. He had made it plain she ought to marry him. He wanted to get the business of a wife and an heir over so he could concentrate on his horses and dogs.

"Have you given more thought to our getting hitched?" Typically, he said the first thing that popped into his mind. Sam was not given to serious reflection.

How like Sam, to think of marriage in terms of

horses and carriages. She would have a gig. She thought longingly of Lord Latham's wonderful barouche.

"Yes, naturally I have. Are you really certain it is what you want? We are not much alike." They were worlds apart. Yet, with all the time he spent out with his horses and dogs, hunting and shooting, she would likely never see him. Except at night. Yet—he was a decent man. He would be a just father, a tolerable husband.

"Nothing more fit and proper. You'll get over the notion of wanting books when you have a few young-'uns to tend. Children will keep you busy, I'll be bound."

Amazingly enough, she didn't blush. His talk did not send her into a swoon as might be expected. Blunt, to be sure. But then, what could she expect from Mr. Ainsworth?

"Fine. We'll get spliced. No rush. Time enough after the hunting season is over next fall." He took it for granted that she'd agree and that her parents would be pleased for her to wed the squire's son.

"Good morning, Miss Herbert. Ainsworth." The baron and Lady Susan paused before them, an inquiring look on her face as she took note of the proximity between them.

"Tabitha and me will get buckled come this fall," Sam announced, sounding self-complacent.

"What?" Lady Susan exclaimed, looking as amazed as she sounded. Lord Latham wore no expression, but his eyes seemed to blaze at Tabitha with reproach. Why she should be apologetic she didn't know. He didn't want her and Sam did.

"Dare I suggest this is rather sudden?" the baron said in a somewhat chiding manner. He didn't look pleased.

"No, no, I been talking to her about marrying for an age. She is never one to be rushed, you see." Sam wore a well-pleased look on his sturdy face that reminded Tabitha of his favorite horse. Or dog. Either one.

Tabitha was thankful she wasn't required to say a word. But . . . what had she done? Wouldn't spinsterhood be preferable to listening to Sam's dull conversation for the rest of her life? It was astounding how stupid one could be at times. But she had not refused and the die was cast.

Lord Latham hustled Lady Susan to her carriage, then walked briskly to his, Sir Anthony with him.

"Well, that's done," Sam declared in his self-satisfied way. "Mama said as how you'd never settle into the life of a squire's wife. I daresay you will. Besides, you'll have Mama to guide you every day."

"We will live with your parents?" Tabitha felt as though she was sliding into a deep hole with no way out.

"Naturally. No sense in getting another house when there is plenty of room with them. Mama could use some help with the preserving and all."

For the first time in her young life Tabitha felt faint. She must do something. Perhaps she could say she had been mistaken? No, that wouldn't do, but there must be some way to undo the stupid harm she had done today.

The baron's carriage pulled away and her thoughts took wing. What a terrible tangle she had made of her life!

"Well, that was a surprise." Hugh lounged against the well-padded cushions of the barouche while he contemplated doing away with Sam Ainsworth.

"Miss Tabitha Herbert, that angelic enchantress with that country clod? Unbelievable," Sir Anthony said with a shake of his head. "There must be some mistake."

"I would have sworn that she had no notion of marrying him yesterday. Why, she talked about her future as traveling around the country to visit her sisters. You know, the doting spinster aunt thing."

"Somehow, I think that Miss Herbert wouldn't remain on the shelf very long. Sooner or later one of her sisters would bring forth an acceptable *parti*. I wonder why she suddenly threw herself at the country clodpole?"

"Ainsworth, drat the man. I don't understand it in the least," Hugh murmured. "I was certain otherwise. What do you mean, 'threw herself'?" he demanded of his old friend.

"While you were walking out, all attention to your betrothed, I was watching our Miss Herbert. She studied the pair of you, turned rather pale, then besieged the clod."

"He is, isn't he?" Hugh barked a laugh. "Although I understand he is first-rate with his horses and has prime hounds for his hunting. I wonder if Tabitha hunts?"

"How could she? Mr. Herbert doesn't strike me as that sort of man. And she, such a lady! In a squire's home!"

"Tony, if I know the lady, she will excel at whatever must be done. Look how well she did with my library."

"She still has to complete her work," Sir Anthony reminded. "Should I seduce her away from the clodpole?"

"Ainsworth," Hugh reminded absently. "No, that

would not do. Pity you couldn't lure Lady Susan," he mused. "Or at the very least interest her in someone else—like West."

"Are you telling me you regret your betrothal so soon? What happened? Did you suddenly realize what a treasure Miss Herbert is and change your mind? Lord, Hugh, you are truly mixed up." Tony gave his friend a scornful look.

"I shall come about. I always do, if you recall." Hugh gave his friend a serious look, slightly challenging.

"I suppose you want a bit of help. All I need to know is *who* is to do *what* to *whom*!" He shook his head in wonder.

They went to the earl's house for a family dinner. When they'd arrived, Sir Anthony said to the others, "Have you heard the latest news? Miss Herbert is betrothed to Mr. Ainsworth. Buckled, I believe he called it. She didn't deny it," he added when Miss Latham gave him a horrified look.

"What is this?" Elizabeth demanded to know as she left the carriage to join them. When told, she cried, "You must be mistaken. I cannot believe Tabby would agree to such." She rounded on Hugh to request an explanation.

"Ask her tomorrow," Hugh said with a shrug.

"Believe me, I shall!" Elizabeth walked off in a huff.

The dinner was an ordeal Hugh could have done without. How could he prevent Tabitha from marrying Ainsworth!

Tabitha didn't sleep well. Her stupidity was nothing to the pained stare of dismay bestowed on her by Mama. Her father looked affronted, but said little.

The squire, after all, was a worthy gentleman and so must be his son.

She was not in best looks when the gig came for her. It was possible she might sneak into the library without anyone being the wiser. She was sole occupant for a brief time. She dreaded the moment she must face the baron.

Septimus found her at once, butting his head against her legs so she would pick him up for a cuddle. "Dear Septimus, I vow you'd never get into such a pickle— at least not on your own." They had never solved the mystery of how the cat came to be shut up in the small basement room.

Septimus purred, his eyes closed in bliss.

"It is all very well for you to look so smug. Your life isn't all of a muddle. Oh, if I could be whisked away from everything." She thought about that with longing. How lovely to forget all that happened yesterday! How could she have been so stupid? She would have to get out of the dilemma, and as obtuse as Sam was it wouldn't be easy.

Setting the cat on the floor, she concentrated on the rest of the books. The large sized volumes had to go into their cabinet. It was a handsome piece of polished mahogany with fine detailing of thin brass in classic designs.

Once she shelved them, she recalled the stack of books and manuscripts in the other room. She carried them to the library with great care. At the bottom was a manuscript that appeared to be of considerable age.

She frowned over the script. She didn't read much Latin; moreover, it had been written with elaborate flourishes.

"Is there some problem?" Lord Latham inquired from over her shoulder.

"Not a problem, precisely." She regarded him with a faint frown. "It is this manuscript in Latin. It appears to be exceedingly old. Possibly it is of great value?" She handed the book to him, and watched as he placed it on the large desk at the far end of the room.

"It appears to be a history of this part of England."

"But that is wonderful!" She ran to join him by the desk, staring down at the ancient book. "You ought to translate this rare work. I'll wager there would be many people who would like to read that."

"What? The parson's daughter betting? I can't believe it." Sir Anthony sauntered into the library, the epitome of a fine gentleman once again in shades of gray.

Miss Latham scurried in behind him, curiosity alive in her eyes. "What is going on? I must know." She also went to the desk, scrutinizing Hugh and Tabitha, then the manuscript. She was as puzzled as Tabitha had been.

"Tabitha has found an old manuscript. It appears to be a history of this area. Here, look for yourself." He moved aside so both of them might examine the fragile book.

"How very old it appears," Miss Latham said, delicately touching the frayed and stained vellum.

"Suppose one of your ancestors wrote this down?" Sir Anthony said with a considering frown. "Hugh, you owe it to him to translate it into English."

"Fascinating work. But I would need help." He glanced at Tabitha. "I'd need someone with a fine hand to write what I translate. Alas, my handwriting is not the best."

Sir Anthony stepped back to study Tabitha, who knew she blushed with both gentlemen looking at her with such expectation. "I doubt, sir . . ."

"Why, you would be the perfect one to help dear

Hugh. It would mean a great deal to the family, my dear," Miss Latham exclaimed. "I am sure that no one could object to such a worthwhile project, least of all your parents."

"It would mean working long hours—together," Tabitha stammered. "I don't think Lady Susan would be pleased."

"Pooh," Sir Anthony said with a flick of his fingers. "I can take her shopping or whatever she wishes. I am willing to do *my* part you may be sure."

"Is there a date on this, Hugh?" Miss Latham wondered while she examined the title page.

"I suspect that once we translate the entire manuscript the date will become obvious." Hugh again turned to Tabitha and she knew that she would not reject his request. She had finished her other work—*this* was doing something truly worthwhile. She never once gave a thought to what Sam Ainsworth might think of the project. She thought only of helping Lord Latham.

"Well—If you think I may be of help, I am only too willing to assist you." She wondered if she had lost her mind. The ramifications of her decision crept into her brain. Surely Sam Ainsworth would have a royal fit about her remaining closeted with Lord Latham for who knew how many weeks. The transcribing would not be a simple matter.

At that moment Elizabeth, Lady Purcell, came drifting into the library, her eyes alight with interest. "I sense there is something going on here. I would know it all."

George followed, keeping a keen eye on his wife.

Miss Latham took it upon herself to explain.

Elizabeth turned a few pages of the manuscript, exclaiming over the ornamental lettering, a reverent finger tracing a few of the capital letters embellished with red ink. "I trust you will keep this in a safe place from now on. I think you *must* translate it. What a fascinating piece of history this must be!"

"Miss Herbert has agreed to assist me."

Elizabeth's gaze darted from one to the other. "Ah, what a perfectly splendid notion. Tabby has a beautiful hand, which you, dear brother, most certainly do not. Your scrawl is almost indecipherable." She sniffed in disdain.

"Such kind words almost unman me, dear sister."

"Oh, pooh, as though you pay the slightest attention to anything I say. But you *are* to transpose this to English? I think once you are done you must place this original with the other treasures in your collection." She folded her arms in front of her, her eyes limpid pools of impishness. "I do think it will be excellent that Tabby is to help you, dearest of brothers. You need help."

Before Lord Latham could reply to this, a sound was heard from the next room. Someone was coming.

"Well," Lady Susan cried from the doorway, "what has brought everyone in here this morning?" She hurried across to where the others were gathered, Jasper West in her wake.

Elizabeth explained. "Tabby found this old manuscript and Hugh is going to translate it. It is a history of this area. I fancy it could be equal in importance to the Domesday Book." She smiled benignly at Lady Susan and Jasper, sure that even the nearly illiterate Susan would have heard of the survey of England ordered by William the Conqueror in the eleventh century. The very vellum upon which this was written signified its age.

"As important as all that?" Lady Susan was clearly impressed. "Well, it is a good thing you do it, for I would never have the patience to figure out what all those strange letters are." She glanced at her cousin, who was scowling at Lord Latham, then at Tabitha. "Could you?"

"Not in the least," Jasper replied eventually.

Elizabeth's smile matched a look Septimus wore when pleased. Miss Latham suddenly assumed a highly virtuous expression on her sweet face. Sir Anthony's eyes gleamed.

"With the permission of Miss Herbert's parents she will assist me. As Elizabeth claims, my handwriting is not the best." Lord Latham grinned at Tabitha. Any thought of Tabitha's backing out of the undertaking vanished.

"What will your Mr. Ainsworth have to say to this!" Lady Susan demanded to know.

"I have not the slightest idea," Tabitha replied with more composure than she thought she possessed. "Besides, we are not wed as yet. He cannot have any complaints to voice if my parents are agreeable."

Lady Susan frowned, giving thought to this turn of events. "I suppose that is true."

"Well," Lord Latham declared, "I think this is cause for celebration. Let's go to the drawing room for a glass of champagne." He placed the vellum manuscript into a large drawer in the desk, safe from careless maids or Septimus.

With a flurry of conversation, they all strolled to the drawing room, Lord Latham pausing to speak to Crowder on the way to request the beverage.

"You are committed now, Miss Herbert. I shall not let you back down." He walked at her side, glancing down at her. He could almost touch her and fought that urge.

"Providing my parents do not object, I think it will be a rather exciting enterprise. Do you suppose it might be a forerunner to the Domesday Book itself?

The information gathered for Kent by the investigators King William hired?"

"I was too busy looking at the actual writing. The problem will not only be the script, but the Latin. It won't be simple."

"If needs be, we could always ask my father to join us. He is gifted with languages—Latin and Greek."

"I learned Latin, but . . ." He motioned to Sir Anthony. "Tony, you will stick around for a time, won't you? You were always good at Latin. We may need some help. I bought a copy of the two-volume 1783 edition of the Domesday Book and just this year a volume of indices has been printed by the Record Commission. I'll order that for our possible use. *And* I'll brush up on my Latin."

Sir Anthony agreed with a pleased expression.

Crowder entered with a large tray bearing slim glasses and two bottles of the finest champagne from the cellar.

"Here's to our historical endeavors," Lord Latham said by way of a toast. His gaze fixed on Tabitha, seeming to offer a meaning she couldn't grasp however much she might wish.

"Indeed, sir. May we learn a great deal about our past." Tabitha hoped it would keep her thoughts away from her future as well.

Chapter Seven

Tabitha peered anxiously at her father. If he refused to allow her to work with the baron, all might be lost. "What do you think, Papa? Is it not a worthy cause? Just fancy—that book might possibly be the Kentish portion of the Domesday Book! I have learned each shire collected the information individually before it was gathered into the final survey. And this could be for Kent!"

Her father slowly nodded. "I believe you would be performing a worthwhile service. I shall be more than happy to lend any assistance I might offer—in case Lord Latham comes across a word that puzzles him. The Latin of that period can be puzzling as they tended to mingle French with it."

Relieved, Tabitha retreated to the sitting room. Once alone with her mother, Tabitha asked, "Will you manage?"

"I shall have to, dear. Remember, when the day comes that you marry, I will have to do for myself." She smiled warmly to take away any idea of regret on her part.

Tabitha was able to climb into the gig sent for her with an easy mind. Now all she had to do was to guard her heart from a further attachment to Lord Latham.

Upon her arrival at Latham House she found Crowder in the entry hall. The house was utterly silent.

"Is Lord Latham in the library, Crowder?" She pulled off her gloves and closed her parasol. She had little knowledge of Latin, only what she had heard when her father was coaching boys destined for Eton.

"No, Miss Herbert. He and Sir Anthony came down to breakfast some time ago. You might peek into the dining room." He unbent sufficiently to smile at her.

"Is Miss Latham about?" Tabitha enjoyed chatting with the older woman and would just as soon not face Lord Latham before it was necessary.

"I believe she went out for a little walk."

Tabitha thought a minute. If Lord Latham was not to be seen, he obviously wasn't ready for her to write. She would seek his aunt. Pulling on her gloves once again she informed Crowder of her intentions before leaving. Outside she paused, looking about her in all directions. Off in the distance near the lake she could see the slender figure that was unmistakably Miss Latham.

Unfurling her parasol, she walked in that direction. The sun was warm today, which is likely why Miss Latham was strolling along the lake, pausing now and again to enjoy the scene. Tabitha hummed a tune, happy with being where she was and content with seeing Miss Latham.

The old swan was paddling lazily off shore. Tabitha sent him a narrow look. Could the bird tell she neither liked nor trusted it?

"Miss Latham! Good day," Tabitha sang out. She hurried to join the dear lady she admired.

Harriet spun around on the sloping bank. She stepped on a small loose rock and cried out as her ankle appeared to give way. Arms waving frantically in the air, she lost her balance and tumbled—right into the lake and far too close to the swan for Tabitha's comfort.

It didn't take more than one scream to bring Tabitha dashing. She kicked off her slippers and tossed her parasol aside. Harriet sputtered to the surface. Tabitha suspected she could easily walk out, but it appeared the older lady was confused and shocked by her precipitate plunge.

Tabitha jumped in, heedless of the proximity of the cob or the depth of the water—which was greater than she realized. "Miss Latham, take my hand and I'll get you safely ashore." She extended her hand, which Miss Latham grasped, nearly pulling Tabitha under in her eagerness to get to dry land.

The swan had its own ideas, it seemed. It swam close, and adopted a menacing posture as though intent upon attacking the women. It drew back its elegantly carved neck and arched its upper wings. The loud explosive grunting call was quite enough to frighten the hardiest of souls, let alone a foe! Tabitha risked her own balance by splashing water at the swan and trying to shoo it away.

Miss Latham appeared—just for a few moments—as though she might faint from the fright and threat.

"Please, do not swoon on me," Tabitha begged.

The older lady nodded, flopping an arm about as though trying to assist in their passage to land.

Tabitha dog-paddled—alternately dashing water at the swan—until her toes could touch bottom. Then she towed Harriet Latham from the lake. They both scrambled up on the grassy shore, sitting a few moments to catch their breath and gain a measure of calm.

"How fortunate there was no one to see my ignominious splash!" Miss Latham said with a rueful grimace, standing as soon as she was able. Her blue jaconet gown dripped a trail of water as she took a few steps. Gazing down at her drenched self, she shook her head sadly. "We are both a sight. Pray that no one sees us." She wrung water from the hem of her gown. Tabitha did the same, regretting the damage to her dress.

Harriet slanted a narrow glare at the cob. "The swans are supposed to be mute, but that noise was enough to send any gently bred woman into a fit of the vapors."

Tabitha stuffed her feet back into her slippers, then picked up her parasol. "Come, it may be a mild day, but I'd not wish to see you take cold."

Harriet Latham didn't need any coaxing. The two hurried up the slope to the house. Crowder opened the front door, his eyes nearly popping from his head at the sight of the two bedraggled women.

"Towels, Crowder. And be so kind as to send for my maid. We had a minor disaster." Miss Latham wrung out more water from her gown before entering the house.

Tabitha said nothing. She was wondering what in the world she was to do. Her clothing was at home, naturally. Perhaps she could summon the gig to take her there? She risked a chill, but what else to do?

"Good heavens, what happened?" Elizabeth sped down the stairs to join the two women. "You fell in the lake, I suppose. You poor dears! But how?"

"I fear I called out to Miss Latham and when she turned to see who was coming, she lost her balance and tumbled into the water," Tabitha replied. "Poor lady! That old cob was close by and gave us quite a fright, let me tell you!" Tabitha shivered, feeling ridiculous.

"I ought not have been so close to the lake. Such

a lovely day, you know," Miss Latham said vaguely. "The water was chilly and that swan menacing. I'd not like to meet it in the water. Or anywhere else, for that matter."

"Hugh ought to get rid of it." Elizabeth joined Miss Latham and Tabitha where they steadily dripped water. Two little pools collected at their feet. Tabitha suspected her slippers were quite ruined and her dress might never be the same again. She would need an entire wardrobe at the rate she was destroying her clothes!

"The cob thought we were encroaching on his territory and took great exception to us!" Tabitha accepted a large towel from Crowder. Miss Latham wrapped the length of linen about her that her maid had rushed down for her use. She looked surprisingly elegant in the draped fabric.

Tabitha gently touched Miss Latham's arm. "I am so sorry this happened. I'd not have had you in the water for anything in the world."

"Well, my dear, at least you didn't stand there bleating with helplessness. You knew at once what needed to be done and you did it. I told you it would be a good idea if you learned to swim." She started for the stairs.

"But I didn't," Tabitha whispered. "Learn to swim, that is."

"Truly?" Miss Latham paused to stare back at Tabitha. "Then you are a heroine, rushing in to save a foolish old lady as you did."

"What is this?" Hugh Latham inquired as he came from the dining room, followed by Sir Anthony. "What happened?"

Tabitha was doubly thankful that she had draped the large towel about her. Imagine having the men see her—again—with her garments plastered to her body.

"You explain, Tabitha. I am going to my room." Miss Latham marched up the stairs with her maid at her side.

"It was like this," Tabitha began, giving a succinct account of what had occurred. "I am so sorry I startled Miss Latham. I'd not have had this happen for the world. She was terribly frightened."

"The old cob, Hugh." Elizabeth gave him a penetrating stare. "One of these days that bird will truly attack someone and then you must do something."

"Mute swans are known for getting along well with people," he countered. "Why, I've even fed them from my hand. I think you are making a great fuss about nothing." He turned to Tabitha, taking note of the spreading pool of water at her feet and her little shivers every now and again. "Elizabeth, perhaps you can assist Tabitha?"

"Of course, dear brother mine. How silly of me, I should have had you upstairs at once. Come with me, Tabby. We are of a size and I have just the thing for you."

Hugh watched the two go up the stairs before heading to the library. "Perhaps we can begin to work on that book." He and Tony sauntered into the library, having enjoyed a good breakfast and quite ready for anything.

"What about the swan, Hugh? Tabitha seemed quite afraid of it. Are you so sure there is no danger?" Sir Anthony crossed the room to look out at the lake.

"Well, I suppose if you are in the water and you can't swim and that great bird comes at you looking like it is ready to attack you might be alarmed. But there is nothing to fear on dry land. I doubt if Miss Herbert will go near the lake again, or at the very least, not in it." Hugh pulled the drawer open to withdraw the large book.

"If you say so, old man." Sir Anthony strolled to the desk to look down at the first sheet of vellum. "Do you always call her Miss Herbert? I should think she would practically be a member of the family after all this time."

"Elizabeth calls her Tabby. Somehow I think of that for a cat. Tabitha is not a cat by any means."

"I've known a few of those and your sister isn't one either. Nice lady, your sister. What about your marriage to Lady Susan? Is it on or off?" At Hugh's sudden stare, Sir Anthony shrugged, and said, "Just wondering. Tabitha is a lovely girl. I could do much worse for myself."

"I had no notion you were even thinking of getting married, Tony." Hugh frowned at his friend.

"Susan is far too admirable a person to be taken as second best. I got the distinct impression that you felt you had made a mistake in your proposal." Tony bent to examine the first page of the book, tracing a large letter with a tentative finger. He did not meet Hugh's eyes.

"Perhaps you should flirt with her, then," Hugh said.

Sir Anthony gave Hugh a speculative look, then grinned. "I won't tell what I intend to do. Let it be a surprise."

"Around here?" Hugh gestured to the large room and the house beyond. "Nothing remains a secret around here for long." He smiled, then turned his attention to the book on the desk. He sighed. "This is not going to be simple."

"Few worthwhile things are," Tony replied. "I suspect you will be glad of Tabitha Herbert's help. Let's begin."

Up in Elizabeth's room Tabitha shivered as her gown was taken away to be dried along with her petticoat and shift. She wrapped the damp towel about her again. The maid handed her a petticoat and a shift of fine cambric to don.

Elizabeth bustled into the bedroom from her dressing room, carrying a gown of soft violet.

"Do not tell me that is another mistake. I'll not believe you." Tabitha smiled at her friend.

"No, not a mistake, rather a gown that I will not wear for so long that when I can, it will be out of style."

"Never say you are . . ." Tabitha wondered aloud.

"Indeed, I am in a highly interesting condition, as my mama would have said. You may as well wear this and take it home. Before I leave I shall give you a few others." Elizabeth shook her head, a look of mischief in her eyes. "Is that not dreadful? Having to obtain an entire wardrobe after the babies are born?"

"Babies?" Tabitha accepted the pretty gown of soft mull, slipping it over her head with the help of the maid.

"The doctor says it will be twins. They run in our family, you see. I have twin uncles and twin cousins. Whoever weds Hugh had best be prepared for possible twins."

"Mama would say it is the fastest way to have a family." Tabitha straightened the dress, admiring the delicate flounce at the hem and the prettily puffed sleeves. "I heard of one lady who had three sets."

"Of twins? Dear me!" Elizabeth exclaimed, sinking down on the bench at the foot of her bed. "Perhaps I shall just have the one set. That would do nicely, better yet if they are girl and boy." She sat for a moment, then rose. "Come, we had better return you to Hugh. He will be impatient to begin work on that book." Elizabeth led the way from the room to the stairs. She smiled fondly at George as he came up the steps to her side.

"Do I see another gift?" he said with a kindly look at Tabitha while reaching his hand out to his dear wife.

"And why not? I will need an entire new wardrobe within the year." She gave him a saucy grin.

"I had no idea babies were so expensive." He guided her along the hall and they disappeared into their room.

Tabitha cast a wistful glance back at them, then made her way down the stairs and into the library. Taking note of the open book she asked, "Have you begun?"

"I sent Tony to hunt out my Latin grammar. We ran into words we didn't recall. I think it is in the schoolroom on the top floor. One puts schoolbooks aside as soon as possible." He studied her, then said, "I see Elizabeth has lent you a dry gown. Er—that color suits you well."

"She gave it to me, as she claims it will be out of style by the time she can wear it again." At his raised brows, she added, "Did you know that Elizabeth is expecting twins? How curious that they tend to run in your family."

"Elizabeth is in the family way? She said nothing to me about it. A mere male is left out of all the interesting goings on," he complained.

"Perhaps I should not have said anything. She gave me this dress, explaining that she wouldn't be wearing it for quite some time. I appreciate her kindness more than I can say." Tabitha smoothed her hand over the soft mull fabric, content in the knowledge that it became her well.

"But I doubt you need charity. Your father has an independent income and he is not badly paid."

"True," she said recalling her sister Priscilla's lament about Papa not getting the bishopric he deserved.

"Is something wrong? You look rather distressed."

"Nothing of importance." Tabitha took herself in hand to concentrate on the work. Seating herself behind the desk, she sought and found a pot of ink and several of his excellent, and quite new, steel nib pens. "Paper?"

Lord Latham joined her behind the desk to extract a pad of paper from a bottom drawer. He squatted down to get the paper and he was just a little below Tabitha's head as he looked up at her. "You are determined on this marriage to Mr. Ainsworth? Somehow you do not seem an equal match. I cannot see him ever reading a book."

Stung by his charge on a highly vulnerable point, Tabitha attacked in turn. "I imagine it is quite as sensible as you marrying Lady Susan—who doesn't even read!"

"That is nothing to do with you!" He rose to stare down at her, anger clear in his eyes.

"I agree. My match with Sam Ainsworth has nothing to do with you, either. As the son of the local squire, he is considered a catch by all the local young ladies."

"His mother as well?"

Tabitha took a deep, calming breath. She preferred not to think about that dominating woman. "I am not marrying her." She avoided meeting his astute gaze. He saw too much.

"I understand you are to live with his parents." His lordship toyed with a paperweight while studying her.

"Goodness, how people do love to gossip." She studied her hands where they rested on the desk.

"Yes, we are supposed to live with his parents. I hope to alter that."

"And how, pray tell? I think him quite content to leave you to his mother while he and his father are out on their horses with the dogs. I'm told he dotes on his dogs."

"And that is so unusual in a country gentleman?" Tabitha bestowed what she hoped was a cool look on his lordship. She ought to call off her betrothal. More and more she saw trouble ahead. But how could she?

"What does he say to your coming here to assist me?"

"He has said nothing regarding it." If she thought her betrothed ought to take umbrage at her working so closely with a handsome baron she wasn't about to say anything to that effect. She doubted Sam Ainsworth would ever reveal jealousy about anything! He wouldn't care at all. If that thought stung, she would keep the fact to herself.

Sir Anthony walked into the library, thus ending what had become a very uncomfortable conversation for Tabitha. Book in hand, he strolled over to join the tense pair who were at the desk. His smile grew, and one brow raised in what Tabitha thought a rakish manner.

"Ah, what a ravishing creature we have with us, Hugh. I vow, my father's secretary is a poor sort of chap. How envious Papa would be should he see Miss Herbert. Miss Herbert, my compliments." He captured her hand, and placed a kiss, not above it as was usual, but directly on her sensitive skin.

Flustered, and not truly displeased, Tabitha hastily withdrew her hand from his. "You, sir, are a flirt."

"But, my dear, *you* are a feast for the eyes." He glanced at Lord Latham to add, "Has Lady Susan seen her dressed like this? No, I don't suppose she has or things would be changed and you would find yourself with the same dull sort of fellow that my father employs."

"Perhaps we might begin? That is, if you are finished with flirting?" Lord Latham smoothed his hand over the vellum page, his smile seeming a trifle strained.

"But Hugh, I am never done with flirting! I might as well give notice to quit." After this dramatic statement Tony subsided, opening the Latin text to prepare for work.

They had satisfactorily translated the opening pages of the book, now convinced that it could well be the work they hoped it to be, the precursor of the Domesday Book, when sounds came from the entry hall.

"I'd wager that is your betrothed, Hugh. Oh, I shall enjoy this." Sir Anthony crossed his arms, quickly taking refuge some distance from the desk so it appeared that Hugh and Tabitha had been working alone.

"Well, and here we are, come to cheer you in your efforts," Lady Susan caroled as she entered the library, closely followed by Jasper West. When she spotted Tabitha at the desk with a surprised Hugh standing at her side, she stopped in her tracks. Her mouth formed a perfect O.

Tabitha rose and came around the desk to drop a faint curtsy. "Good day, Lady Susan. I trust all is well with you?" Tabitha inquired politely. She doubted that Lady Susan would be the least put out at Tabitha working with Lord Latham. But on the other hand, she thought it prudent to put some distance between Lord Latham and herself. Blast that Sir Anthony for his teasing.

"I am fine," Lady Susan enunciated crisply. "I can see you are in fine fettle. What a lovely gown you wear. Is it new?" She walked slowly forward, eyeing the soft violet mull with a doubtful expression.

"Actually, it belonged to Elizabeth. I, er, had an accident this morning. She came to my rescue with this dress, as I was desperately in need of dry clothing."

Sir Anthony sauntered forward to Lady Susan's side. He lazily captured her hand to place a light kiss well above it. "Tabitha is our heroine. She rescued Aunt Harriet from a watery grave, or the assault of that cob swan. Either way, that lady was very thankful. Tabitha's a very handy woman to have around."

"Quite," Hugh replied while taking note that Tony still held Lady Susan's hand, however lightly. He also noted his betrothed's flashing eyes. Being a sensible man, he turned to Tabitha to suggest an end to their workday. "We have a good start. Perhaps we can do more tomorrow?" He gave her an assuring smile when he saw the worried expression in her eyes. "I am pleased with what you have done so far. You are a very organized person."

"That comes from helping my father, who is anything but organized." Tabitha edged around them toward the door.

"You will have to show your mother how to do that before you marry Mr. Ainsworth. Or do you intend to return home from time to time to help him?" Lady Susan spoke politely, with no edge to her voice. Yet Tabitha sensed she was suspicious of the relationship between her and Lord Latham.

Before Tabitha could reply Aunt Harriet bustled into the room offering a smile to one and all.

"Why do we not all enjoy a bit of nuncheon? It is such a lovely day, I persuaded Crowder to arrange things on the south terrace. Come, it will be lovely," she commanded sweetly. She took Tabitha's arm, thus cutting short any idea of her departure.

Lady Susan could be heard gently berating Lord Latham for not offering to take her to the local assembly.

"My dear lady, you should know Hugh never goes." Sir Anthony grinned impudently at Hugh. "*I* shall devote my evening to you. It will be a pleasure, I assure you. Surely you know what a dull dog you are to marry? I'll wager you'll not get him to London for the Season."

It didn't take much to see this displeased Lady Susan.

Chapter Eight

"My Lord, Mr. Ainsworth is here to see Miss Herbert," Crowder intoned, making it clear in a subtle way that he didn't precisely approve of the chap.

"Show him in, Crowder." Turning to Tabitha, Hugh added, "Likely your intended has come to see how you fare."

"Mr. Ainsworth must join us for our nuncheon," Aunt Harriet insisted. "I have yet to meet this gentleman."

When Sam Ainsworth entered the library he found six pairs of eyes fastened on him with disconcerting intensity. Once at Tabitha's side he said, "You are surely finished with this nonsense by now, ain't you?" He didn't bother to lower his voice, not caring if he insulted anyone. His face was innocent of malice. He looked bored.

"Oh, it isn't the least nonsense, Mr. Ainsworth," Aunt Harriet declared firmly in a frigid voice. "This is an important undertaking, one dear Tabitha performs with great skill. Hugh could not manage without her. How fortunate her father approved her assistance with this momentous task."

It was evident that Sam Ainsworth did not like to have his grumbling ground cut from under him.

It was equally clear to those who knew her that Aunt Harriet had taken Mr. Ainsworth into instant dislike.

Lady Susan stepped into the sudden silence. "La, Mr. Ainsworth, perhaps you care to join us and learn more?"

When Sam focused on the dazzling figure of Lady Susan he appeared quite taken with such awe-inspiring beauty.

Well, thought Tabitha, Lady Susan was enchanting in a gown of sunshine yellow, trimmed at the bottom with four narrow double flounces edged with lace. Her delicate bonnet was trimmed with yellow and white silk roses. Sam might be forgiven if he was struck dumb at the sight.

Tabitha had forgotten her own newly acquired gown.

Sam spotted it at once. "*You* are fine as five pence this morning." He almost looked affronted, as though Tabitha had no business in dressing so finely.

Tabitha just barely kept from gasping. Had Sam sneered at her? She replied with a ladylike "Thank you." After a moment she asked, "What is it you wish to see me about?"

"I went to your house and you weren't there," he complained. "Your mother said you were at the baron's house. I thought perhaps you were finished with this poppycock." He gazed about with mild curiosity, totally unaware that he had offended the baron.

Tabitha was ready to breathe fire.

Obviously, the sight of so many books failed to excite any curiosity. Now, if a book had been about breeding horses he might have perked up. As it was, he had no interest. None at all. Tabitha wondered if he had the slightest interest in *her*, other than as a means of securing the Ainsworth line. What a lowering thought!

Lord Latham suavely persuaded Sam to join them on the terrace. "Surely, old chap, you must eat. Do join us. I should like to know the next squire a little better."

Although Tabitha was certain Sam had broken his fast, she also knew he never refused food. He would grow to be like his stout father, she reflected. Naturally he acquiesced to the nuncheon.

Sir Anthony fell in beside him, asking about Sam's latest purchase, a chestnut hunter of impeccable ancestry. Sam was pleased to expound on something worthy of his concern. He spoke at great length about something he liked.

In the flurry of all leaving the house and settling at the table on the terrace Lord Latham came up to Tabitha.

"It seems he doesn't mind you being with me. He appears to think that what we do is of no importance." He glanced at Sam. "I cannot think he is the man for you."

"That is not for you to decide, is it?" she stated. She slipped past him to sit by Elizabeth, making certain that she and George had been introduced to Sam.

"So, at long last I am to meet your betrothed." She studied Sam with a considering eye, circumspect but thorough. "He is a sturdy gentleman," she concluded at last. She turned to examine Tabitha with curious eyes.

Tabitha thought it a very tactful description. How discreet Elizabeth was. Lord Latham had said he thought Sam wasn't the man for her. And who, pray tell, would he suggest as being "right" for her anyway? Surely not his friend, Sir Anthony. He looked as though he was interested in Lady Susan. And as for Mr. Jasper West, she had never in her life met a man who had so little to say. He was like a shadow that followed Lady Susan about wherever she went.

Mrs. Dolman had excelled herself. The food was tasty. Tabitha observed that while Sam might not approve of what Lord Latham did, he had not the slightest problem with enjoying his hospitality. He ate well of every dish.

Following the meal, Sam excused himself.

Tabitha thought it incumbent upon her to walk with him to the door. "I feel I must remain here as long as Lord Latham requires my assistance," she said. She wondered if Sam would try to persuade her to leave.

Oddly enough, Sam turned a benign smile on her, one she hadn't seen before. "I think this book business a lot of bother, but I don't mind you being here. After all, it ain't likely that a man of the baron's position will look twice at *you*. You are as safe as in church."

"Really!" Tabitha didn't know whether to laugh or throw something at Sam. Instead she clamped her lips shut and saw him out the door. Her mind whirled with the insults she longed to hurl at Sam's dense head. How dare he think her so lacking in attraction that Lord Latham would take no notice of her! Then she raised her head to see that very gentleman in front of her. Her cheeks burned with chagrin. She wished herself a million miles away. How humiliating!

Lord Latham stood just off to one side of the hall. There was no way he could have missed the insulting words Sam had uttered. She knew he must have heard every word, for Sam was not given to speaking quietly.

"Well? I imagine you overheard what Mr. Ainsworth just said. I doubt he intended it to sound as it did." Her excuse for Sam's heedless words was lame and she knew it.

"You cannot marry that man, Tabitha. He does not deserve you. You are an enticing, sensitive creature. He would trample on all the finer feelings you have."

Tabitha could scarcely argue with that sentiment. She felt the same way. Yet her honor compelled her to deny the thought. "I imagine that he believes that since I am the daughter of the rector I would be above flirting with you."

"That is not what he meant. He said *I* would not be attracted to you. And there he is wrong. Dead wrong."

"That is all well and good, but . . ."

The baron barred her way, touching her chin lightly with his finger. He gazed down at her with an intensity she found unnerving. "You deserve a man who is devoted to you. He should not look kindly on your spending hours with me. I would never permit a woman I loved to be with another man for any length of time—no matter how innocent the reason. It could lead to an attraction they could not deny. I could kiss you and would he care? I doubt it."

As though to demonstrate his point, he gathered a bemused Tabitha in his arms. He placed his lips lightly on hers in what was probably intended to be a slight touching of lips to make his point.

Only it didn't work out that way.

Tabitha felt as though she were aflame. A fire singed her nerves, tingled through her veins, melted her spine. She responded like a bird soaring to the sky for the first time, hesitant, then gaining power, and finally exultant at the flight that had been achieved. She had longed for this and yet had not known it.

At long last Hugh stepped away from the passionate young woman and the kiss that was unlike anything he had experienced in his life, feeling as though he had been hit over the head with the very pole he had wanted to smite Sam Ainsworth with. Stunned.

They stared at one another in silence—for what could be said? He dropped his hands from her shoulders. Had he really kissed Tabitha Herbert in such a fashion? And had she truly kissed him back?

"Tabitha," he began, only to be silenced by a shake of her head.

"Best to say nothing of this at the moment. I daresay neither one of us has a sensible thought in our heads." She retreated a step, then walked passed him looking amazingly composed. He trailed behind her, his own thoughts chaotic.

"There you are Hugh," Lady Susan caroled gaily. She stood close to Tony who wore a smug smile. That neither of them was looking at the book scarcely penetrated Hugh's mind at the moment. He was still badly shaken.

"I have chosen to remain with the sunshine," Tony quipped while looking fondly at Lady Susan.

"Tabitha saw Mr. Ainsworth off." Hugh knew he couldn't have managed to say more than that at the present.

If Tony thought it had taken a considerable amount of time to bid Sam farewell, he said nothing. Only Hugh knew the look in his eyes and thought it promised mischief.

Lady Susan lost interest in the ancient book almost at once. "I insist you go for a walk with me, Hugh. It is a fine day and I am tired of spending so many hours in the house." Her pout was a delicious moue and her eyes crinkled up delightfully.

"But Lady Susan, poor old Hugh is committed to

this undertaking." Tony darted a gleam of challenge at Hugh. "He will not rest until he has translated the entire book. Allow me the pleasure of your company, my ray of sunshine."

Hugh nodded. "He is right, my dear. Enjoy a stroll along the lake with him. Taking care not to fall in the water, of course," Hugh concluded, with an attempt at humor.

Once they had departed after much teasing upon Lady Susan's part, the room fell into total silence.

"Tabitha," Hugh began, "I scarce know what to say—except I ought not have prevailed upon you in such a way."

"I think you ought not have sent Sir Anthony off with your intended." Tabitha turned to look out of the tall window behind them. In the distance Lady Susan's yellow gown and Tony's tall figure showed clearly. "He seems rather attracted to her. If you do not take care, you may lose her. What would the earl say then?" Tabitha glanced back at him, her blue eyes full of questions.

All Hugh could think of was the way the light picked up shimmers of gold in her silver gilt hair and how sweet her lips tasted, quite as though they longed for another kiss. Which, he reminded himself, was not to be considered.

"Let us cross one bridge at a time. Perhaps if we concentrate on the translation, all will come about?" And pigs might fly. Hugh knew he could *not* remain betrothed to Lady Susan, not when he felt the way he did about Tabitha Herbert! And could she actually marry that clod, Ainsworth? A man who held his horses and dogs in higher esteem than the woman he planned to wed? Never!

Aunt Harriet and Jasper West entered the room from the terrace, deep in a discussion of the habits of swans and other aquatic fowl. In particular they spoke of the cob.

"Dear Mr. West thinks we ought to do something about that cob swan, Hugh. It could have attacked me, you know."

Hugh smiled, relieved to have a change of topic. "I doubt anyone need to worry about that bird. What harm could it do? I can't imagine anyone who couldn't outrun a swan."

Aunt Harriet sniffed her displeasure, and suggested Mr. West join her in the garden to see the topiary.

After they had left the library Hugh turned to find Tabitha safely seated behind the desk, copying down what he had translated earlier in her neat hand. It was as well. Perhaps they could resolve the issue between them later.

What a tangle this all was. How could he get Tabitha to break her engagement to Ainsworth while at the same time induce Lady Susan to end their betrothal? There had to be a way without making either of them appear indiscreet.

"Aunt Harriet wishes to do a bit of entertaining while she is here and we have Elizabeth and George as well. Once they go home, it is likely to be a long time before they return." Hugh studied Tabitha's down-bent head, enjoying her glorious hair without worrying that someone was taking note of his pleasure.

"And then, God willing, with the twins." She glanced up at him, her eyes amused.

Hugh shook his head. "I still cannot believe that my scamp of a sister is soon to become a mother."

"Most women do, once married."

Hugh caught her dry smile and laughed as likely intended. "I suppose so. But twins!"

"Your wife might have twins as well, you know."

The thought of Tabitha having children with a man like Ainsworth brought a sinking feeling. Not wishing to dwell on the awful possibility, Hugh took the book to the desk and began to translate an account of a long-ago estate from the obscure Latin with its peculiar mixture of old French.

Then he recalled the dinner. "What I wanted to do before we were side-tracked was to invite you to dinner. And your parents as well, of course." He waited, impatient for her reply, willing her to accept.

Her expression became cautious. "Thank you. I must ask Mama." She dropped her gaze to the papers on the desk. "Do you think it wise?"

"We are neighbors. Your father is my rector and you are . . . my friend, are you not, Tabitha?" She seemed the staid Miss Herbert no longer after that kiss that had sizzled through him from top to toes.

He could pretend they were merely friends. Surely no one could quibble. After all, she was his transcriber. They were half a room apart—most of the time. And heaven knew when someone would come wandering into the library. It was open at all times. They were safe.

"If you wish me to be your friend, I am honored."

Some time later Tabitha looked out of the window to see Lady Susan and Sir Anthony strolling up the lawn toward the house. If she knew anything at all, Sir Anthony had been flirting with the lady. From the pleased smile on her face, Lady Susan did not find his attentions the least objectionable. Was that the sort of wife she intended to be? To wed one man and continue to flirt with others?

"Your Lady Susan returns with Sir Anthony. He seems to be quite the charmer. At least," she amended, "he certainly has charmed Lady Susan. Look for yourself." Tabitha did not wish to make trouble, but Lord Latham ought to discover which way the wind was blowing.

Lord Latham left the old book for the window. "It is as you say. Tony enjoys a bit of flirtation. Most men do."

"You as well, I take it?" That momentous kiss was merely a bit of flirtation. She had best remember that. It was a salutary lesson for a green girl from the rectory.

He turned to stare at her. "I could say I am only human. On the other hand, it might well be that the entrancing creature I kissed led me to discard all notions of propriety or manners." His eyes met hers, a hint of a smile lurking in their brown depths.

Little sparks danced up and down her spine. Vexed with herself, she turned her thoughts to how to disentangle herself from the engagement to Sam. How had she been so stupid? No matter what, she couldn't marry Sam. Lord Latham didn't know the half of it. He had never met Mrs. Ainsworth.

The discussion ended when Lady Susan and Sir Anthony entered, bringing with them a breath of fresh air.

"La, what a beautiful day!" Lady Susan cried, beaming at Sir Anthony, then Lord Latham and Tabitha. She carried a furled yellow parasol and waved it about.

"It is, indeed," Sir Anthony agreed.

Lord Latham took the parasol from his betrothed before it hit the figurine on a nearby table.

"Tea!" she declared. "I am perishing for a cup of tea." To Tabitha she added, "Do you not find yourself in need of refreshment after a vigorous stroll?"

Vigorous stroll? That to Tabitha was a contradiction. She rose from her chair. "I'll let Mrs. Dolman know."

"Is something wrong, Miss Herbert?" Sir Anthony

inquired, his eyes sparkling with impishness. "Do not tell me that Hugh stepped out of line. I'd not believe it."

"Lord Latham is all that is proper, sir." Perhaps that was true and it was Tabitha who had yielded to temptation? For the darkly handsome and tall gentleman was most assuredly the most tempting creature alive. She skirted past his lordship to escape from the library. Fortunately she found her quarry at once.

The housekeeper was not the least surprised at the request for tea. She was taken aback that Tabitha had come to find her to make the request.

"You could have rung, miss."

Since there was no way that Tabitha could explain that she had ardently desired to leave the room and those who threatened her peace of mind, she merely smiled. "I thought if I found you it would save you time and steps."

"A thoughtful young lady you are, to be certain. Your mother can be pleased with you, she can."

Tabitha knew she must promptly return to the library or the others would think it strange behavior.

She entered the room, observing at once there was a strained silence. What was afoot?

"Lady Susan wishes to attend the assembly in Tonbridge. Do you plan to go?" Lord Latham asked Tabitha.

"No. That is a trifle far. I doubt I could persuade Papa to take the time."

Lord Latham turned back to face Lady Susan and his friend. "It isn't practical. No moon, for one thing."

"Oh, Hugh, be reasonable. It would be such fun!" Susan turned to clutch Sir Anthony's arm. "Would you take me? And Jasper, of course."

"Why couldn't your cousin escort you?" Lord Latham asked. Tabitha wished to know as well.

"A cousin! I want someone else for an escort." She fluttered her lashes first at Hugh, then at Sir Anthony, who raised a brow in inquiry.

"Could you not leave that fusty old book for one evening?" she said with a stamp of her slippered foot. "I cannot see how Tabitha can bear to keep you company if you are going to be such a dreary spoilsport." Lady Susan turned to Tabitha. "Would you not like to go? I adore dancing." She pirouetted around, her skirts belling out around her so she looked like a bright yellow tulip.

"I shall take her. I see no reason why she cannot go," Tony declared. "I have a comfortable carriage with good lamps. My man should be able to find the way without difficulty." Again he sent a look of query to his friend.

Lady Susan resembled a little girl who has finally had her way and looked enormously pleased. "There! I shall surprise you, dear Sir Anthony. I have the prettiest new gown to wear."

"I shan't guess, other than to wonder if it is yellow." Sir Anthony strolled across the room to lean against the fireplace mantel. From here he could survey everyone in the room. Tabitha noted he watched Lord Latham the same way a cat studies a mouse before it pounces.

"No! It is green, but beyond that you must wait." She sailed up to Lord Latham, plucking at his sleeve with an impatient hand. "I vow, you will be sorry."

"I trust all will turn out well." He removed her hand.

"What a strange thing to say, Hugh dear." She continued across the room to where Sir Anthony lounged against the mantel, a picture of a man who knew every trick in the book—far more than the young woman in yellow.

Tabitha watched in fascination.

"You will pick me up early, will you not? I cannot bear the thought of missing a single dance." Her pout was adorable, but Tabitha thought that had she been a child she would have been sorely tempted to paddle her bottom.

He nodded. "I'll be in time. Hugh will give me all the necessary details."

Lady Susan giggled in a most enchanting way. "How vastly amusing. My affianced giving directions to the gentleman who will take me out. Well," she said looking at Hugh, "you cannot say we are clandestine about anything!"

"No, I cannot."

Tabitha thought he looked guilty and wondered if anyone else interpreted his expression as she did.

"Where is Jasper? La, he is never around when wanted. And too frequently found when not!" Susan grinned impishly.

Tabitha answered, as it appeared Lord Latham was deep in thought. "Your cousin went with Miss Latham to view the new topiary in the garden."

"Oh." Lady Susan showed no interest in another garden.

"I could send for him," Lord Latham offered.

"Are you trying to get rid of me?" She laughed, secure in the knowledge that no man would feel that way.

"Of course not. I merely thought that if you intend to go to that dance in Tonbridge you might wish to return to your house now so you could be ready on time."

She darted a hasty glance at the longcase clock that stood at the far end of the room. "That is true. How thoughtful you can be when you wish. Have Jasper summoned so we may leave at once." Her command had an imperious ring to it and Tabitha admitted she looked rather queenly.

He crossed to summon Crowder, adding, "Your carriage will be called for as well. I'd not want to be the cause of your missing a single dance."

"Then you ought to take me," she said, reverting to her earlier attempt at persuasion.

"Not this time." Lord Latham looked over her lovely head to meet Tabitha's gaze.

She couldn't imagine what message he sent. But there was little doubt it intrigued her!

Chapter Nine

•

When Tabitha offered her the nicely written invitation to say Mrs. Herbert was taken aback put it mildly.

"Goodness! I am quite overwhelmed!" Mrs. Herbert stared at the hot-pressed cream paper in her hand with an air of surprise. "It will be nice to see the work you've completed. But to dine with the earl and countess!

"I think it very gracious of the baron to include us," Mrs. Herbert added, reading the invitation a second time.

Tabitha could almost see her mother mentally reviewing her wardrobe. "We have two weeks, Mama. Perhaps the mantua-maker could create something simple in that time. And there is some of the beautiful lace Nympha gave us."

"But the earl and countess will be there—Lady Susan's parents. I cannot think why *we* are invited." She gave Tabitha a perplexed look.

"Perhaps Baron Latham appreciates the help Papa and I have given him on that book he translates." Tabitha had no idea what prompted his invitation, but she would attend—even if she had to suffer seeing him with Lady Susan.

Just how Tabitha could end her own engagement

without causing a major rift between her family and the squire, she didn't know. Not that *Mrs.* Ainsworth would care in the least. To consider sharing a house with her was beyond Tabitha's ability to endure, far worse than Sam.

It was not comfortable to continue to work at the baron's house. True, Latham Court was quiet what with George insisting that Elizabeth's behavior be subdued. But too many hours were spent in proximity to the baron, hours that were not easy for Tabitha, feeling as she did. The past week had held numerous difficult moments.

Aunt Harriet, as that lady insisted Tabitha should call her, bustled here and there in the house, preparing soothing and tasty potions for Elizabeth as well as something to perk up Tabitha.

"You are sickening for something, my girl," she declared with far too knowing a manner.

"Nonsense. I believe the Latin is beginning to affect me." Tabitha smiled, pausing while she recorded a line from the translated text.

"How so?" Aunt Harriet tilted her head like a slender bird listening for a mate's call.

"I feel as though I am slipping into an ancient world." Tabitha added quietly, "Mrs. Ainsworth has made it plain that what I do is unacceptable in her eyes."

"What a pity Sam Ainsworth didn't settle on some docile creature who would permit his mother to guide her as *she* sees fit." Harriet bestowed a shrewd look on Tabitha.

Tabitha had no idea how to reply to that. Actually, the more Tabitha considered the matter, the more she realized she would have to think of a very clever way to extricate herself from this predicament so that everyone involved would be satisfied.

Sam needed a wife and had thought Tabitha suitable. His mother wanted someone more malleable. The trick would be to find another woman—respectable, willing to adore Sam no matter what, and agreeable to Mrs. Ainsworth. It would help if the girl liked dogs. Horses, as well. However, that could be overcome if necessary.

Tabitha cast her thoughts to those young unmarried women in the area who might fit that description and came up with a blank. But, please God, she did want someone soon! It might be coming onto midsummer now, nevertheless autumn was approaching and then it might be too late!

Lady Susan was a problem of a slightly different sort. She strongly opposed the time her betrothed spent translating the ancient book. No matter how often he explained to her the value of such an under-taking, she shrugged it off. He should be available for her whenever she desired an escort—which was rather often.

It appeared to Tabitha that the lady had a bit of a temper. She hadn't missed the sparks of fire in Lady Susan's eyes when the baron rejected some scheme of entertainment that she thought quite fine. Mr. West stepped in more often than not to calm the troubled waters.

Several days before the day of the dinner, Susan breezed into the library where the baron and Tabitha worked. "What a nitwit you are, to spend these glori-ous days in this dreary room," she snapped to Lord Latham to his obvious displeasure. "Warmer weather is here—the two of you remain in this dusty old room, cooped up like hens!"

Her accusation annoyed Tabitha so much that she spoke before thinking. "He is scarcely a fool if he can translate that archaic Latin with its smattering of odd French."

Lady Susan gave her a speculative look and frowned. "Well, I can't imagine who will be interested in that rubbishy thing." Lady Susan paced about the room, her yellow gown flowing silkily about her restless form.

Lord Latham looked up from the book he patiently translated, and bestowed a weary smile on her. Pencil in hand he considered her a moment, then said, "I imagine there are any number of scholars who will eagerly lay siege to the book once I am done."

"It is the outside of enough! I insist you take some time to amuse me. What is the point of being engaged if we do so little together?" Her pout was too clever by half.

Tabitha thought Lady Susan had a point. It seemed that Lord Latham avoided escorting his betrothed anywhere, other than church. He refused to attend the assemblies in Tonbridge, nor had he suggested a picnic or any other form of amusement for her pleasure. The only forthcoming delight for Lady Susan was the dinner at Latham Court.

Tabitha hoped the dinner might appease her. Somehow she rather doubted that pampered young lady would be gratified. It seemed Lady Susan thought only of herself and her wants. She might be gloriously lovely—she was also selfish. Would she ever come to appreciate Lord Latham as he deserved to be esteemed? Only time would reveal that.

Elizabeth confided that Lady Susan thought twelve a paltry number for a dinner. "But I think it quite fine," she declared. "I enjoy a small party far more than a crush. Actually, I believe five couples best, seating is more evenly arranged. But Hugh insisted upon the guest list."

"There is so much for Lady Susan to enjoy in this

house—his paintings, the silver, all the other collectibles he has." Tabitha waved a hand at the magnificent collection of paintings and priceless sculptures here as well as in the drawing room.

"True. I fear Lady Susan may not appreciate them. She dislikes all these ancestral portraits, you know. Calls them dreary. She insists that she and Hugh must remove to London for the Season every year. Hugh may not like that. He wishes to be here at planting time—to supervise."

"I fancy that if you love someone enough, you would be willing to make adjustments in your life." Tabitha wasn't sure there was that much love on either side, but then what did she know? That lone kiss Lord Latham had given her might have transported her to bliss and merely satisfied a whim on his part. She didn't like to think that of him, but she was a rather green girl, when all was said and done.

The day of the dinner dawned to fine weather for a change. They had endured far more than normal rain and with that, chilly temperatures. Today seemed more like a summer day—or, at the very least, a fine spring day.

Elizabeth had complained that she was still wearing her winter gowns and was heartily tired of them, while Aunt Harriet draped at least two shawls about her slender shoulders as she bustled about the house. They would assuredly welcome airy summer fabrics. Only the crouching cat topiary had welcomed the wet weather—filling out the form with leafy green—looking more and more like Septimus.

Tabitha had taken to using a shawl as well. The footman kept the library fireplace burning all day long, a cheery glow compared to the otherwise dismal, sodden landscape beyond the windows. Her new gown of fine sarsenet would be best viewed if not hidden under an enormous shawl.

"I hope the rain holds off," Mrs. Herbert said with an anxious perusal of the sky.

"The clouds do not look as though they will pour forth at the moment. Perhaps the rain will wait until tomorrow?" Tabitha prayed so as she considered her pretty new gown. The thought of being soaked in the rain was horrid.

When it came time to dress there was still no rain. With a glad heart Tabitha donned her lavender sarsenet gown with its fetching puffed sleeves. Fastening a strand of pearls around her neck, she thought she could face Lady Susan knowing that she was quite up to snuff.

"Remember the earrings, dear. They will finish your costume quite nicely." Mrs. Herbert crossed to the dressing table to find the elusive items before handing them to Tabitha to put on. "I must say, the mantua-maker did an exceptional bit of work on your gown. The adaptation of the design we saw in *La Belle Assemblée* turned out very well."

"I like the mulberry jaconet you chose. We shall be as fine as five pence, dear Mama."

"I do not in the least dread dining with Miss Latham and the baron, even Lord and Lady Purcell. It is the earl and countess that I confess put me in a quake. And Lady Susan—as an only child she has been much indulged. Pity, that." Mother and daughter exchanged meaningful looks.

"Lady Susan may a trifle pampered, but she is a sweet person for all that. Miss Latham said the earl and countess are very pleasant people and not at all high in the instep." Tabitha drew on her gloves, suspecting she sounded more optimistic than she actually felt.

"Well—heretofore my only dealing with them has been at the church door." Her mother's anxious frown revealed that Tabitha's kind words had not truly relieved her mind.

With this uncertain remark, the two women hurried down the stairs to where Mr. Herbert awaited them with patience developed over many years of living in a household with far more women than men.

Mr. Herbert took the baron's offer to send the barouche for them as a sign of gracious condescension on his part. Mrs. Herbert reveled in the luxurious vehicle. Tabitha wondered why his lordship had done it.

Crowder welcomed them into the house with his usual stately dignity—and a kind smile for Tabitha.

"Welcome, welcome," the baron said in his rich, deep voice as he came forward to greet them. He shook hands with them all, drawing Tabitha with him to the drawing room where the family and Sir Anthony gathered. He didn't hover at her side, rather tending to her parents instead.

Sir Anthony left the warmth of the fireplace to meet Tabitha and her parents, although the elder Herberts merited little attention from him. When the baron ushered her parents to where Miss Latham and Elizabeth sat, Sir Anthony remained by Tabitha. He chose to flirt lightly with Tabitha, teasing a smile from her.

"La, sir, it would seem you are a trifler." She gave him a sly smile, fluttering her lashes as she had watched Lady Susan do with such effectiveness.

"It would seem you can tease as well, fair one."

He was never to know what she might have replied as the earl and countess, Lady Susan and Jasper West entered at that moment. All attention focused on the newcomers.

The Countess of Montfort wore a stunning creation of silver gauze over peach satin appropriate for an evening in London. The earl was more modestly garbed. His attire fit in quite well with what was worn by the other gentlemen.

Tabitha approved his neatness of dress before turning her attention to Lady Susan. That young ladyship's silver and primrose-figured sarsenet gown had silver bows decorating the line of the low neckline and around the hem. She looked utterly enchanting. And knew it.

Sir Anthony left Tabitha's side to speak with the earl, offering his excuse to her with polished grace.

Elizabeth greeted the arrivals with her gentle warmth, supporting her older brother in an unobtrusive manner. Miss Latham also joined the reception, seeming well acquainted with the countess. The rector and Mrs. Herbert fit in nicely, offering the inevitable comments on the weather.

Jasper West sauntered up to where Tabitha stood nervously fingering her fan.

"You look as though you ought to be attending Almack's rather than a country dinner," he said, bowing politely.

She gave him an assessing look. "*You* are here, so it cannot be too countrified. I daresay we are all quite the thing tonight." She repressed a desire to grin at him.

"Well done. As to a country dinner party, I trust you will not find it as dreary as the weather has been." He glanced around. "I do not see your betrothed. Is he not to come? Or is he late?"

"He will not be here this evening." Tabitha didn't know why Sam had been omitted—but she was thankful.

Elizabeth drifted up to the pair, offering witty conversation. Tabitha took the opportunity to glance to where the countess and Lady Susan stood conversing with Miss Latham and Mama.

Say what she would, Tabitha's mother held her own very nicely in a well-bred manner. There was nothing that Tabitha could detect to give the countess contempt of the rector's comely wife. She might not have a gown worthy of London, but she did extremely well for a country dinner.

Sir Anthony rejoined Tabitha, cutting out Jasper with a subtle method that impressed her.

"That was not kind, Sir Anthony," she said so softly only he might hear.

"And when has anyone ever said I was *kind*, pray tell! I'd far prefer being called dashing and arrogant."

"Well, as to that, may I suggest you have all qualities? You have been kind to me, even if you are somewhat arrogant to others. As to dashing . . ." She studied him, then glanced at the other men. "I should say you could put a London dandy to shame."

"A hit—a palpable hit!" He laughed at her quip, causing Jasper West to stare at them.

"We attract the attention of Mr. West. He looks exceedingly annoyed. Have we violated some minor edict of Society, sir?" Tabitha discreetly held her fan before her to prevent her words from carrying very far.

"Minx. You must know that Mr. West considers himself an arbiter of manners. I would guess he thinks it ill-bred for us to laugh as we do." Sir Anthony gazed down at Tabitha with a highly speculative expression in his eyes.

"As to that, I enjoy laughing on occasion. I suggest Mr. West ought to laugh more and pass judgement less. I believe it might agree with his digestion better."

Sir Anthony gave her a half-smile, his eyes held a trace of puzzlement as he scanned her face.

Before she could investigate why that might be, Crowder summoned them all to dinner.

The baron escorted the countess. Lord Purcell accompanied Lady Susan, while Sir Anthony walked with Elizabeth. Jasper squired Mrs. Herbert, leaving Mr. Herbert with Tabitha in the move to the dining room. Aunt Harriet, as her nephew's hostess, walked to the dining room on the arm of the earl, offering conversation that made him smile.

Tabitha slipped onto her chair, casting a questioning glance at the baron at the head of the table. She sat between her father and Jasper, which was difficult. She had no problem talking with Papa. On the other hand, Jasper made her uncomfortable. She had the oddest feeling that he constantly weighed her, judging everything she said or did. She hoped he would spend much of his time chatting with Sir Anthony, who was on his other side.

The earl sat between Elizabeth and Aunt Harriet while Lady Susan was on the baron's left and the countess on his right. Papa would have to spend some minutes conversing with her, but Tabitha didn't think he minded in the least. The countess was a handsome woman.

Six couples necessitated an uneven arrangement. She could understand why Elizabeth thought five couples better. Tabitha would by far rather have sat next to Sir Anthony—if she couldn't be next to the baron. She observed that Lady Susan appeared to want the baron's entire attention, which couldn't be, given that her mother had first claim. Even when the countess chatted with Papa, it seemed to Tabitha that the baron was preoccupied and not paying much heed to Lady Susan—poor dear.

When it came time for the women to leave the table to the men and their port, Tabitha gladly hurried behind Aunt Harriet and the countess. Elizabeth joined her, catching hold of Tabitha's arm to chat about the countess's spectacular gown. Lady Susan slipped off in the general direction of the water closet. Tabitha gave her not the slightest thought. It wasn't proper to comment on people who disappeared to answer the call of nature.

The countess summoned Tabitha to her side. "I hear you write out the translation that Baron Latham makes from that old book. Is that not tedious for a young girl like you?" In the countess there were signs of the same beauty found in her daughter, the same imperious character as well. It was like seeing Lady Susan as an older woman. Tabitha's heart ached for the baron. She could not foresee a happy future for him, wed to Lady Susan.

"Not at all, ma'am. I find it fascinating to read about *who* lived *where* in Kent so very long ago."

"I fancy the Montforts were mentioned?" The countess preened a bit, secure in the antiquity of her husband's lineage.

Tabitha supposed she was entitled to her superior mien. "I have yet to come across the name, but no doubt you are right." She glanced at Lady Susan who had silently slipped back into the room.

Shortly, Lady Susan was at the pianoforte playing a pretty piece, the sort girls trotted out for company.

The men joined them at this point. Tabitha was surprised, thinking that they would linger over their port far longer than they had. She turned to study them.

The earl was speaking as they entered the drawing room. "I should like to see that book, Latham. Sounds like a dashed fine undertaking. You are to be commended for such perseverance—in spite of what some people think." He glanced at his wife.

"By all means, let us have a look." Mr. Herbert

added to the earl, "I have helped out from time to time when Tabitha brought home a word or phrase that was hard to puzzle out. She copied it out for me, you know. The original is far too precious to leave the library. I shouldn't think but what it could be listed as one of the more valuable books in the country!"

"Well, now! I must see this, Latham. Never say that book was in the house all these years and you knew nothing of it?" The earl gave the baron an incredulous look.

The men began walking from the drawing room, the baron explaining how the worn, old book had been at the bottom of a pile in an ignored corner of a cupboard.

The moment he entered the library Hugh saw the book was gone. Vanished. He had worked on it just this afternoon! "Gone! I cannot believe it! How can it be?"

"What is it? Something is wrong, I gather." The earl queried with a frown.

Hugh explained, "The book was here earlier and now it has gone missing."

"Oh, I say, Hugh, it simply can't be missing," Sir Anthony protested. "For one thing it is rather large. For another, who would take such a thing!"

Jasper West sauntered to the window, staring out into the twilight. He checked the door. "Well, this is firmly latched. How about the windows?"

"One is always cracked open to keep the fireplace from smoking when the wind is this direction. All the others are shut." A sense of panic crept over Hugh. Surely no one would take something like a dusty old book? It was a rare item, true, but how many would know that?

"I'll ask Miss Herbert if it was here when she left

earlier." Tony nodded to Hugh before leaving the room.

Hugh went to check the large drawer of the desk where Tabitha usually sat while writing. Perhaps she had put it away—fearing a servant might damage it. Only her copy was to be found there.

"What is it, Lord Latham?" Tabitha Herbert cried. "Sir Anthony was so mysterious when he asked me to join you."

"Have you seen the book?" He stared at her, hoping she had tucked it in a safe spot.

"I assure you—the translated copy is safely in the desk drawer." She paused near the fireplace to look at the table where Hugh had spent so many hours— near and yet so far away from her.

"The original book has disappeared."

"Where could it be?"

"I was hoping you might be able to tell me."

"You surely do not think I took it away!" She looked both frightened and insulted if such a thing was possible.

"No, no, I put that badly. I am having a hard time thinking clearly. I hoped you might have put the book in a safe place." His eyes beseeched her, hopeful, expectant.

She shook her head. "I have not been near it."

Lady Susan had slipped into the room, and now stood next to her cousin Jasper. "What a pity. Now you won't have anything to occupy your hours." ·

Jasper gave her a questioning look.

"Well, if he has nothing else to do, he can always accompany me to an assembly or even shopping."

The silence following her inane remark was so complete that the crackling of the fire was the only sound to be heard.

Chapter Ten

The evening fell apart after the dramatic scene in the library. Before leaving the room they again hunted around. It appeared the book had been spirited away!

Tabitha knew every book in the room. "It is no use," she said at last, putting her candle back on the desk. "It is not on any shelf, nor in a drawer large enough to contain it. The fact of the matter is, my lord, the book has vanished into thin air."

"I wonder why air is always called thin?" Sir Anthony mused quietly.

"I suppose you might say it is a bit thick here at the moment, given the situation," Mr. Herbert replied grimly.

"Oh, very good, sir," Sir Anthony murmured.

The earl looked about, his gaze lingering on his daughter, then his nephew. "I suppose we may as well return to the drawing room? Not every host can offer a first-rate mystery to his guests, Latham."

The baron managed a tight smile at this attempt at raillery while escorting the earl from the room. He tossed a look at Sir Anthony as though to tell him to make sure the others followed. No one was to remain. Hugh summoned Crowder to query the servants. Perhaps someone had a clue.

Sir Anthony shut the door on the now empty room. "A bit like locking the barn door after the horse has been stolen, what?" he murmured to Tabitha.

"Truly." She understood why the baron wouldn't want anyone there. It was like the scene of a crime—that is, something had been stolen and he would want to go over the room come morning and better light. She walked with Sir Anthony, while Lady Susan and Jasper West went before them.

"I do not see how a large book can simply disappear, do you?" she whispered, feeling as though the matter too serious to discuss in normal tones.

"No. Whoever took it had a peculiar reason. How many know of its existence or value?" Sir Anthony wondered softly. They approached the drawing room with somber faces.

"Well, what did you think of Tabitha's find?" Elizabeth gaily cried as they entered. Her eyes grew puzzled as she took note of their serious expressions, the concern on her brother's face.

"It is gone." Baron Latham shot his sister a troubled look. "Vanished. Tabitha located the translated portion, but the original book is nowhere to be seen."

Elizabeth rose to her feet with a cry of distress. "But how? All the servants know the importance of that book." She turned to Tabitha. "It was there when you left this afternoon, true?"

"I seldom venture to the other end of the library where Lord Latham is. I believe the book was there. I usually gather up the pages I have done and tuck them in the wide drawer before putting the cap on the inkpot and cleaning my pen. Then I leave."

Jasper spoke at this point. "Why do you remain at opposite ends of the library? I should think you would have to confer with one another from time to time."

Tabitha knew she blushed. "I have learned to read

his hand. I believe he prefers not to be disturbed in any way lest he lose his concentration. It is not the easiest of tasks, you know. One must be a scholar of some degree to successfully do a difficult translation such as this."

"Miss Herbert is correct and she generously does not take me to task for being such a bear about the silence." Baron Latham's expression was rueful. "When those scribes toss in their notion of how some word is spelled it can be rather confusing. They were nothing if not creative. Quite often the name of a town they record bears little resemblance to the present day counterpart."

Mr. Herbert turned to the earl. "I have had to consult Latin texts just to help him out from time to time."

"Of course, the language of those scribes who came here would have been that used at the French court. There weren't all that many who could write," the earl added. "Hadn't thought of that. It is hard to understand why someone would slip into the library and make off with that exact tome. What could they want with it?"

The stillness in the room was complete.

The clink and rattle of the tea tray broke the uneasy silence. Crowder entered with the magnificent silver tray laden with the tea urn, the dishes, and cutlery. The maid following him carried an equally fine silver platter that had plum and Madeira cakes, dainty biscuits, and other delicacies.

Gradually they began to discuss the theft. The countess nibbled at a slice of Madeira cake while expressing her concern for valuables in general. "True, that book was sitting where anyone might snatch it. But think! That could be said of the priceless porcelains and these paintings as well." She waved a hand about at the various treasures displayed in the room.

Mrs. Herbert shook her head. "It is a sad day when something so culturally important is stolen. Surely there is a way to ascertain that the book isn't sold to some unsavory character to peddle to the colleges or scholars."

"Just hope that it is not damaged or destroyed." Tabitha managed to sip her tea, but had not the slightest appetite for cake or biscuits.

"Well, I cannot see why everyone is so concerned. The world has spun around for years without the book. Would it really be that vital?" Lady Susan cocked her head, looking at Tabitha, then to Lord Latham, insouciantly indifferent.

Tabitha shook her head in dismay. How did one explain the treasure contained in the old volume? Why, the history therein was priceless. A knowledgeable thief would gladly steal it to sell to the highest bidder. But *who* that might be was beyond her guessing. She turned to Lord Latham. "You must contact Oxford and Cambridge, the various history scholars as well, not to forget the dealers in rare books. A collector like Earl Spencer would relish such a book."

Hugh nodded. "The rare book dealers first, perhaps."

Jasper set his teacup on its saucer with a clink. "Perhaps the thief will demand a ransom?" He picked up his quizzing glass to swing it idly in his hand. "If the book is so valuable, why not?"

"He'd know he might reap more from a book dealer. This is a one-of-a-kind original, rare, priceless." Hugh wished they would all go home, yet he was aware that perhaps one of them might have something worthwhile to contribute.

"Well, if that is the case," Lady Susan said with a

sniff, "I wonder that you left it out in plain sight where anyone could whisk it away."

"Obviously I did not expect to have it stolen." Hugh gave her a look. Wishing he had locked it away didn't help now. He might have known she'd not be commiserating.

"Susan, that was not a sympathetic thing to say," the earl cautioned, giving his daughter an admonishing look.

"Well, I have heard of nothing but that book for weeks and I, for one, was getting rather bored with it." She flounced from her chair, walking to the fireplace with a decided toss of her head.

The earl looked to Jasper, then the countess. "I believe it is time we bid you good evening, my friend. You have had a shock. We best go."

Aunt Harriet rose. "The first dinner party we have had in ages, and to be spoilt by such a goings on. I declare, what is the world coming to?"

This intriguing topic was discussed for a time until the Montfort carriage awaited them in front of the house.

Aunt Harriet escorted the earl and his family from the room. Hugh followed, watching Lady Susan converse softly with her cousin, her brown curls touching his head.

They made a handsome couple. Pity *they* didn't marry. He must give Susan the idea that marriage to him was the most boring thing to be found. He'd thought his work on the book would discourage her. All she had done was complain and nag—oh, politely and sweetly—but it grated. Now he wouldn't have the book as an excuse to avoid her demands.

Aunt Harriet joined him in the return walk to the drawing room once the Montfort party had gone. "Who do you think took the book?"

"I truly have no idea at the moment. I will go over the room in the morning to see if any clues can be found."

When they returned to the drawing room they found the Herberts standing as though to leave. Tabitha was speaking quietly with Elizabeth and George, while Mr. and Mrs. Herbert conversed with Tony. Hugh went back to the hall to request the barouche be ordered for the Herberts.

"This is a sad ending to the evening, sir," Tabitha said to Hugh, her manner subdued. "I feel like I have been at a funeral, all is so solemn. I suppose you will let me know if there is anything I can do? Otherwise, I shall stay at home, awaiting word. I confess I shall fret every moment, wondering what is going forth!" She chewed at her lower lip a moment, then added, "I should like to help."

"I will send the gig for you first thing in the morning. After all, you originally found the book and if anyone knows this library, you do. Why, I can't think of coping without your help." Hugh hoped he hadn't overdone it, but he truly wanted her here. Just her presence was a balm to his anxious mind.

"Very well, I shall be here first thing, then." She joined her parents on their way to the entry. Hugh walked with them, as did the others. "It will seem very strange not to be transcribing those long ago particulars," Tabitha said sadly. "Let's hope a good sleep will help our hunt."

Hugh saw them into the barouche, then stood watching as the carriage went down the avenue toward the village.

"She will be back tomorrow." Tony nudged him in the arm. "So glad you remain engaged to the lovely Susan. I believe I'll see if I can wrest the exquisite Tabitha from the unworthy arms of her betrothed.

Ainsworth does not in the least deserve that treasure of a girl."

"I can agree with you on that last sentiment. But you don't strike me as being ready to settle down and marry, my friend." Hugh stifled the urge to tell Tony that he had better leave Tabitha alone or else.

"Who said anything about marriage?" Tony said in a joking way. "On the other hand, think how delighted my mother would be with Tabitha. The daughter of a respected rector would please her no end. The grandniece of the Earl of Stanwell is not something to sneeze at, wouldn't you admit?" He grinned at Hugh, his eyes full of mischief.

"I have long thought so." Hugh resisted the desire to plant Tony a facer, went in the house and along to the drawing room. He couldn't endure the library tonight. He poured a brandy for them both, George having seen Elizabeth to their room, with Aunt Harriet retiring at the same time.

"Who could have crept into this house and taken that book while we were at dinner?" Hugh wondered. "It had to be when the deed was done. There are too many servants around before and after dinner. Dinner is the one time when the footmen are occupied with the serving and the maids scurry back and forth. There would have been sufficient bustle and noise to cover a stealthy entrance through that window."

"Perhaps tomorrow things will look better? Maybe Tabitha saw something when she left the dining room?"

"One can always hope," Hugh murmured.

"It is a fine thing when something like that precious book is stolen right when the house is full of guests!" Mr. Herbert declared over his breakfast.

"I suppose it would be the easiest," Tabitha inserted.

"True, dear," agreed Charlotte Herbert. "Think of the noise the servants make, although they try to be as quiet as may be. They are concentrating on bringing the food up from the kitchen at the greatest speed without spilling anything. It is a wonder the meals arrive as warm they do. That is one good thing about a small house, dear. The kitchen is not a country mile away from our table."

"Charlotte, my dear, you have never complained. I did not realize the reason!" Mr. Herbert smiled benignly at his wife before heading off to his study.

Tabitha had just tied on her new villager hat when the gig from the Court drew up before the rectory. She hurried to the carriage. Rain looked eminent, but thankfully it was still holding off.

Bowling along the avenue leading to the main house Tabitha gazed off at the lake where the swans could be seen serenely floating about. The old cob was there, as were the others, plus a scattering of ducks. She would like to stroll along the lake, admiring the scene, given time.

Once at the house, Crowder welcomed her with a grave expression. "His lordship awaits you in the library, Miss Herbert. I shall bring tea shortly."

"Thank you, Crowder." She looked at him in sympathy, handing him her umbrella, gloves, bonnet, and pelisse.

"'Tis a sad day here, make no mistake." He took her things, shaking his head as he did.

"I know," she murmured before hurrying along the hall and into the library, smoothing her hair as she walked.

"At last! I thought you would never get here.

Come—join me over here where we can study the room. I need a fresh pair of eyes. Mine do not see anything amiss."

"Perhaps that could be a clue—that nothing is amiss. Think. You had the book on that table. What of your writing paper and pencils? Nothing is out of place, is it?"

"True, but I don't see what that could mean."

"Well, it tells us that whoever came knew precisely where to get the book without disturbing a thing. None of the books on the shelves have been disturbed or misplaced."

Hugh nodded. Strolling about, he stopped before a window at the far end. He stared at the bottom of the window while rubbing his chin. "The odd thing is that the window is precisely as I left it yesterday afternoon. Wouldn't you think a thief would *not* bother about that?"

"How clever to think of that!" Tabitha joined him. "You are right. I should think a thief would be so intent upon escape he wouldn't close the window. Once away from the house he wouldn't worry about discovery."

A footman entered to add coal to the fire, and outside a drizzle began to mist over the parkland.

"It's raining," Tabitha said quietly. "How appropriate. Rain and sadness seem to go together."

"Strange, a few weeks ago I had no idea that book existed." Hugh took a step closer to her. "Now—it has assumed such importance."

Crowder entered at a stately pace, carrying all necessary for a comforting cup of tea plus pastries.

"Eccles cakes!" Tabitha cried. "For that we may be thankful, my lord. Once they were banned as being sinfully rich. No more, I'm pleased to say." She helped herself to one of the crisp, plump, current-filled buttery pastries with their hint of cinnamon and citrus. She savored a bite. "Delicious."

Hugh motioned for her to pour tea, and they settled on the comfortable leather chairs by the fireplace to drink their tea while studying the room and its contents.

Tabitha suddenly recalled Lady Susan slipping off after they left the dining room and before they entered the drawing room. The very notion was preposterous. Still—she would have had plenty of time in which to conceal the book. Why she might do such a stupid thing was beyond Tabitha until she recalled the unfeeling reaction the young lady showed. She had resented every moment the baron spent with his precious book, wanting his attention for herself.

"You have thought of something. What?" the baron demanded.

"A mere idea. Before I make an accusation I would want to explore this room some more and perhaps the room next door as well." She took another bite of her Eccles cake, acquiring a dusting of sugar on her upper lip that Hugh longed to remove one way or another, preferably by a kiss.

That would send her away, for certain. A gentleman minded his manners. A maid entered the room with an offer of more hot water. Hugh smiled, albeit a trifle grimly. Crowder was seeing to it that a servant was in and out frequently, no doubt concerned with propriety.

"There you are, my dears," Aunt Harriet cried upon entering the library. "What a dreary day. Oh— Eccles cakes. One of my favorites." She summoned the maid to bring more china and fresh tea. "I shall join you. Have you thought of anything?" She gave Tabitha an anxious look.

"Nothing of moment. I have an idea, but it is so

far-fetched I shall say nothing until I have done some more exploring." Tabitha took a sip of her cooling tea.

Hugh wanted to shake her. How could she keep him in suspense like this? Unless—"Do you think the thief did not enter the room from outside? Could it possibly be someone who was in the house?"

She shook her head, taking refuge in another bite of her pastry. At last, when she appeared to have given some more thought to this idea that had popped into her head, she said, "Anything is possible, my lord. We must not have a closed mind about a solution or we may overlook a clue."

Aunt Harriet acquired a thoughtful expression, then exchanged a significant look with Tabitha. Hugh wished he could read what was in their minds.

"Precisely what I was about to say," Aunt Harriet declared. "Hugh, dear, why is that window open? There is a decided draft from it that is causing the smoke to come into the room." She gave him a helpless look that meant one thing. She wanted him to leave so she could whisper to Tabitha regarding her notion of the thief. Hugh obliged.

"I wonder if you are thinking what I am? Lady Susan was rather slow to join us last evening after we left the dining room, was she not?" The whisper just reached Tabitha where she perched by the fire.

Tabitha slowly shook her head. "I should not like to think it of her." She met Aunt Harriet's knowing gaze with a grimace. "It would be a dreadful thing, wouldn't it?"

At that point the baron rejoined them. When the tea and pastries had been consumed, the baron recalled something that required his presence at the other end of the house.

"Has he gone?" Tabitha asked as she went to a cupboard that had been ignored last night.

Aunt Harriet peered out into the hall, then turned to nod. "You are safe for the moment. What can I do to help?"

Tabitha didn't answer. She was busy opening the cupboard doors to inspect the insides. "Well, perhaps it wasn't such a good idea. There is no sign of the book here." She sighed and gave Lady Harriet a look.

"The next room? There are a number of cupboards in there." Aunt Harriet bustled from the library into the adjacent room with Tabitha at her heels.

The book wasn't there either.

Tabitha walked to stare out of the window. "The rain has stopped. I do not seem to be able to contribute anything. Perhaps if I take a walk something will come to me. I do not wish to believe that Susan could do such an unkind, underhanded, cruel thing."

"Neither do I. Yet, the book is missing and she was the only one who seemed unaffected by it. Almost pleased, if you consider what she said."

"She has never liked Lord Latham's work on the book," Tabitha reminded. "But to do something like this?"

"Stranger things have happened." Aunt Harriet walked with Tabitha to the entry.

She stood at her side while Tabitha donned her light pelisse, new hat, and gloves and, her mind full of the problem at hand, forgetting her parasol. "I shall see you later on. Perhaps something will come to me while I am out. I will walk along the lake. What could be more conducive to contemplation?" She let herself out, waving to Aunt Harriet before heading in the direction of the lake.

The swans were across the lake. At least, most of them were. Of the old cob, she saw not a thing.

She walked slowly, considering what she believed had happened. Sure as anything, Lady Susan—in a fit of pique—had slipped into the library when Tabitha had thought her headed to the water closet. Where she had hidden the book was a puzzle that might take some thought.

Continuing to mull the matter over in her mind, picking and discarding possible sites one by one, she paid little attention to where she was. The air was fresh after the slight rain. She paused to stare across the sparkling water. A rustling sound alerted her to the presence of another. She spun around, wondering who was here. She didn't see a soul. Then the cob came charging around a bush and straight at Tabitha, a menacing look firing his eyes.

"Shoo! Go away, you nasty old bird!" Tabitha turned and ran. The bird gained on her. She fled—utterly terrified. As large and ungainly as it appeared when on land, it was not slow when it was angered and charging.

Tabitha's long, straight skirts hampered her. She stumbled again and again. The bird drew closer.

A tree root tripped her. She fell forward, hitting her head on a rock. In spite of the pain, she tried to rise. She dimly perceived the bird had grasped her sleeve—and arm—in its powerful beak. She was being dragged into the lake!

"Help!" She wondered if anyone would hear her weak cry.

The water slapped at her as the bird towed her into the water. Encumbered by her skirts, her feeble efforts to free herself were in vain. Twice the swan held her under the water. She tried to escape, but the bird pulled her further out into the water. Her last thought before slipping into insensibility was that she would never see Hugh again.

In the house, Hugh asked his aunt where Tabitha had gone. When he learned she was at the lake, something urged him to find her, bring her back. He opened the door and thought he heard a cry for help. Could it be?

Not pausing to wonder why, he ran to the lake, noticing at once that Tabitha was nowhere in sight! Suddenly he spotted a commotion in the water near the rim of the lake.

The sight of her in the clutches of the cob stopped him briefly. Then he tore across the grounds and into the water, not pausing for a thing until he had her in his arms. Safe.

Chapter Eleven

Hugh dragged Tabitha away from the cob, smashing the bird's beak with his fist to free her from its clutch, then staggered up the bank with her cradled in his arms. He set her down gently to assess her injuries and to catch his breath. Never in his life had he run so fast.

"Tabitha!" he said urgently. "My love, my precious. Can you hear me?" For a moment there was no movement. She lay like a waxen doll. No color stained her cheeks, her hair curled wetly about her head, her bonnet a sodden ruin.

She gave a faint moan. Seconds later her eyelids fluttered, and he gathered her close to him again to carry her to the house. She needed warmth and care! The bundle in his arms was all too still and silent to be pleasing.

Crowder gasped in horror when Hugh strode into the house with his fragile burden. "Milord!"

"Summon Mrs. Dolman and my aunt to the blue bedroom—have them join me. Send a groom for the apothecary."

"At once, my lord." The portly butler marched off to seek out the housekeeper before finding Miss Latham.

Hugh ran up the stairs, not pausing until he reached the blue bedroom. He managed to turn the doorknob, then kicked the door open.

Tabitha looked so pale, so fragile. He gently placed her on the vast mahogany bed, feeling utterly helpless.

He untied the bonnet, tossing it aside. Then he undid the top button of her pelisse. "My darling, speak to me."

Mrs. Dolman must have sped upstairs with winged feet. "My lord, what happened to the dear girl?" As she spoke, the efficient housekeeper began to remove the pelisse from Tabitha's limp body, clucking and fussing.

"The cob attacked her. I knew he had a bad temper, but I didn't believe him vicious." Hugh was aware he had to leave, yet he didn't want to in the least.

"What has happened?" Aunt Harriet demanded as she whirled around the doorway into the room. "Goodness! Poor darling girl. Hugh, Crowder couldn't tell me a thing. How did this happen?" She joined Mrs. Dolman by the bed, assisting her with the wet clothing.

"The swan attacked her. She was unconscious and under water when I pulled her away." The horror that had hit him earlier returned. "I had best leave— something must be done with the bird." It was difficult to leave, but he must.

Pausing in his room to change out of his sopping clothes and boots, he donned dry apparel with haste. Once dressed, he left his room. He tarried outside the door of the blue bedroom, but didn't attempt to enter. That old swan needed to be destroyed.

Hugh tore down the stairs, but was stopped in the entry by Elizabeth and George.

"Hugh, what in the world is going on? Crowder says you carried Tabby into the house soaked to the skin and unconscious. What happened!" She clutched his arm, preventing him from leaving the house.

He explained—a very brief account in his desire to be gone. "Now I must take care of the cob."

"I told you he was a nasty old thing. We could have swan ragout, but he would probably be as tough as nails." Elizabeth wrinkled her nose, even though many considered the birds a rare delicacy to be greatly desired.

Hugh was not the slightest concerned as to the disposal of the old bird. Rather, he wanted him dead so he could never harm anyone else again. His sister didn't stop him when he headed for the gun cabinet on the lower level.

He went out through a ground floor door, taking his gun with him. At the lake, he saw the old cob. The swan had a nasty gleam in his eyes and swam toward Hugh, head down and back, wings raised outward in attack. Hugh took aim.

One shot and Tabitha was avenged. The gamekeeper came running up to Hugh. "I shall fetch the bird, milord." He glanced at Hugh, grimacing. "What should I do with it?"

Hugh closed his eyes, then fixed a stern gaze on his man. "Whatever you please. I don't want to see it again."

Turning slowly away from the lake, Hugh walked up the slope to the house. If only he had listened to the complaints. He'd been reluctant to believe the bird could be dangerous. It was his fault that Tabitha had been attacked. He'd nearly lost his love—by being stubborn.

Back in the house he handed the gun to Crowder, requesting it be cleaned and replaced in the case. He looked up as Elizabeth hurried down the stairs. She came up to pat him on the arm.

"You eliminated the bird, I trust? I have checked on Tabby and she is restless, which is a good sign. Poor dear, what an ordeal to undergo! Imagine! To be attacked by that enormous bird and unable to get away from it. The cob must have been forty-four pounds at the very least and in a terrible temper to boot. It's our long skirts, you see. It is nearly impossible to run at any speed, especially what would be required in this instance. A man in his breeches would not have the slightest bit of trouble." She made a face at him at his expression.

"Elizabeth, are you telling me that you believe women ought to wear breeches? What a shocking creature you are!"

She wore an arrested look on her face a few moments. "I would wager they would be more comfortable."

Hugh shook his head at his sister's outrageous ideas.

George joined them. "The bird is no more, I trust?" To his wife he said, "Miss Herbert? How is she?"

"I think she will come around," reported his wife. "She has good health and won't be inclined to remain abed. I predict she will be up and about soon."

Hugh absorbed this bit of information and charged up the stairs, determined to learn for himself what her condition might be.

Aunt Harriet answered his imperious rap on the door. "Hush, Hugh! She is coming around just now. You do not want to frighten her with your loud noises!"

He pushed past his aunt to see with his own eyes that Tabitha was indeed on the mend. "Tabitha?"

She turned her head enough to see him. Wrinkling her brow, she murmured, "Thank you." Her eyelids drifted shut and Aunt Harriet urged him from the room, coming with him so they might talk and not disturb the girl who still looked like death warmed over.

"You are no doubt blaming yourself over that bird. No one could have foreseen that attack. I wonder what got into the old swan, that he would do such a thing?"

"We will never know as he won't have another chance. I suspect one of the tenants will have swan stew tonight."

"Nothing should go to waste, Hugh," Aunt Harriet said in a reproving manner. "And swan is a luxury for any tenant. I should imagine that several families will benefit from the death of that bird."

Hugh merely shook his head before taking leave of her.

Septimus met him at the foot of the stairs.

"You've been in hiding, old friend. I know—you're not fond of the ruckus. I understand. Your friend Tabitha is upstairs abed. When she's better you may visit her."

The cat sat back on its haunches, looking at Hugh as though it perfectly understood every word he said.

Shaking his head at the foolishness of having a conversation with his cat, Hugh picked up the animal and carried it with him to the library.

He stood in the doorway, contemplating the room within. Who had come here to steal the book? And how had it been accomplished? A noise at the front door made him retreat a step or two to see what was going forth.

"My lady," Crowder said in hushed tones, "I doubt his lordship is wanting company at this moment. It has been a terrible day around here, let me tell you."

Hugh could see Lady Susan give his esteemed butler a withering look. He waited to see what would happen next.

"Well, no matter. I am here and I wish to see my betrothed." She effectively reminded him that she intended to rule here in time, and he had better remember it.

Hugh decided it was time to intervene. He walked to the entry where he faced Lady Susan, who bristled with annoyance. Jasper stood at her side, silent. Susan gave the cat in Hugh's arms a vexed look.

"Good day, Lady Susan, Jasper. How may I serve you?" Hugh continued to hold the cat. If Lady Susan did not like the animal, perhaps it would annoy her to the point where she might break off?

"Well," she replied, seeming taken aback that he might have heard her, "there is an assembly tomorrow evening and I should like to attend. Take me."

She didn't ask, simply demanded. Her behavior didn't sit well with Hugh, who might have been more sympathetic had she been polite. In his arms Septimus squirmed to be free. The cat had made it plain that he did not like her. It was a mutual antipathy, Hugh was certain.

"I fear I cannot leave the house at present," Hugh said in an impressively soft voice. He intentionally gave the impression that there was major illness in the house.

"What happened?" she whispered in reply, stepping closer, responding to his softly spoken words.

"Miss Herbert was nearly killed by a rogue swan. She is at present recuperating upstairs. She was unconscious when I pulled her from the lake—it was impossible to take her home. Aunt Harriet is with her at the moment."

"Nearly killed?" Lady Susan fastened on the two words of importance.

Hugh nodded. "Indeed."

"Oh." She considered that item a moment, then

said, "I fail to see why you cannot take me to the
assembly. It is not as though *you* have to tend the girl.
First it was the book that kept you home, and now it
is Miss Herbert." She narrowed her eyes, studying
Hugh with a manner he found disquieting. "Do you
not *want* to take me?"

The last thing he wished to do now was escort Lady
Susan to an assembly. He could never say such a thing.

Elizabeth chose that moment to come down the
stairs. She greeted Lady Susan with a solemnity usually associated with a death in the family. "Lady
Susan, good day."

Jasper nudged her. "I think it might be best if we
go to the assembly by ourselves. Looks to me as
though Miss Herbert is in a bad way. Stands to reason
that if she was injured here, they would be concerned
for her recovery."

Lady Susan nodded, for once seeming sensitive.

"Later, perhaps," Hugh said in hope of mollifying
her.

"True. There are always assemblies coming up. An
assembly, a card party, or a tea party constitutes most
of our pleasure in the country. It is so boring! We
shall spend every Season in London, I vow!" Lady
Susan insisted.

"Really? I had not realized you did not share my
love of the country in all seasons," Hugh calmly
replied.

Jasper poked her again. "We had best leave."

The pair departed, Lady Susan rather reluctantly.

"Hugh, I was not going to say a word, but if you
make that woman my sister-in-law I will never visit
you."

"I am tempted to marry her for that reason alone."

"You wouldn't! Would you?"

Seeing that he had hurt his sister's feelings, Hugh smiled at her and shook his head. "I was joking. Never fear, things may be altered before you know it."

Elizabeth regarded him from skeptical eyes. "I hope so. I do like you, brother dear. I want the best for you."

Hugh patted her on the shoulder, then set the cat down. He inquired, "Do you suppose it would be permissible if I see how Miss Herbert fares?"

"Have you sent word to her parents?" Elizabeth countered. "You ought to, you know."

Feeling all kinds of idiot, Hugh went at once to remedy this omission, sending a message and invitation for them to come to Latham Court as soon as they wished.

The draperies in the blue bedroom had been partly closed so that when Tabitha opened her eyes again, it was to dim light, with the pale-blue bed canopy over her head.

"Where am I?" she murmured. She shifted her head restlessly on the feather pillow. "What happened?"

"Easy, my dear," Miss Latham murmured. "You will be your old self in no time. You had a nasty experience with that mad swan." Miss Latham smoothed the silver gilt hair away from Tabitha's brow, smiling gently as she did. "You have a rather nasty bump on your head, I fear."

Tabitha shuddered as she recalled the terrifying moments before she hit her head on that rock. She had been fleeing that old cob. It was like a nightmare— where she was running and running and couldn't seem to get anywhere. The next thing she recalled was Lord Latham talking to her, reassuring her she would be all right . . . and calling her his precious love.

She attempted to sit up. Miss Latham cautiously, but firmly, pushed her back against the pillow, tucking the covers up to her chin.

"You became badly chilled, my dear. It's better you rest now." She placed some wrapped, heated bricks by Tabitha's feet, fussing all the while. When the maid entered with a covered tray, Miss Latham inspected it before placing it on the bedside table.

"This tea might feel good on your throat."

Tabitha smiled when Miss Latham, contrary to what she had said moments before, assisted Tabitha to raise up. She gratefully sipped the warm tea. But when she'd had enough, Tabitha was thankful to sink back onto the comfortable bed and pillows. The near drowning had taken more out of her than she would have believed.

She heard the door open. Miss Latham hurried to meet whoever wanted to enter the room, shushing them.

"I had to know you are feeling better."

Tabitha gazed at Lord Latham. Never had he looked so good to her eyes. He appeared anxious, so she sought to put him at ease. "I shall do fine. Probably would have escaped had I not bumped my head on a rock when the swan tugged at my arm and I fell. It is a nasty bird!"

"It was. I venture to say it will be stew this evening. I trust you will be better shortly."

He seemed so concerned she sought to reassure him. "I will be fine. We must return to the hunt for the missing book. *That* is what is important."

"To tell the truth, I had forgotten all about it in the commotion. Wherever the book may be, it can wait. It's more crucial you be restored to perfect health. At the moment you seem far too pale. We cannot have that!"

Septimus slid around the slightly open door, then leaped up on the bed. He stared at Tabitha before crawling up to snuggle next to her.

She threaded her fingers through his soft fur. When the baron would have taken the cat away, Tabitha shook her head. "I find the cat comforting. Leave him be . . . please?"

"Anything you wish." He stood there by the bed, appearing deep in thought as he studied her. "We have missed you today—all of us. Even Septimus had to see you. I doubt the house will seem right until you recover and return to the library—with me to hand you pages of my abominable scribbling which you so ably decipher."

"Your writing is not *that* bad." Tabitha shook her head at his words. "Just now and again. But we must find the book first." Her attempt at a smile was pitiable.

"I am relieved that this episode with the swan hasn't given you a disgust of the entire estate. You may be sure that I will have the gamekeeper maintain a close watch on all the birds so that nothing like this occurs again."

"I confess I might not be eager to walk along the shore of the lake anytime soon. Have you had any success with finding the book?" she asked, returning to the matter at hand. "After all, I have been unable to join you for hours! You might have found it—or at least a clue?"

"Not a clue. You may recall we decided that it had to be someone who was in the house at the time." He watched her very closely, then continued, "Did you see anything? Anything at all? Aunt Harriet would have it that Lady Susan could have taken the book. Is it possible?"

Tabitha transferred her gaze to the window. It appeared to be drizzling again. What was she to say? Lady Susan was a beautiful woman, if a trifle spoiled by her doting parents. And she was his betrothed. "If I have any suspicions, I would rather investigate them first. I'd not wish to charge anyone without good cause."

"I am tiring you. I'll go now, to come back later on when you have had a nap."

"I should go home. My parents will worry."

"They have received my message by now. I'd not be surprised to see them any moment." He glanced back at the door as though he thought they were already here.

After he left her to sleep once more, he made his way down the stairs and around to the library deep in thought.

Shortly after he renewed his search, he could hear sounds in the entry that brought him hurrying from the room. Tabitha's parents arrived, just as he had foreseen. "I am so sorry to have had to send such unpleasant news. You will want to see your daughter at once. Follow me."

They conversed quietly as they went up the stairs. Hugh escorted them to the door of the blue bedroom. "Stay as long as you please. Join us for dinner. You have no idea how much this has touched the entire household. Your daughter is greatly admired here."

That was certainly the truth. It had also affected him deeply. He hadn't realized how much Tabitha had come to mean to him until he dove into the water to rescue her. When he gazed on her still form, sought to revive her, he had never felt so helpless or so desperate.

He reached the entry hall when Crowder met him with the intelligence that the apothecary had arrived.

"I doubt we truly need him." He walked with

Crowder to the entry where the local man awaited him.

"I just arrived home when your servant came. A near drowning, I understand. What has been done so far?"

Hugh motioned the apothecary to join him as they walked up the stairs, explaining what had occurred and been done. Hugh let him into the blue bedroom, leaving him with Tabitha before taking Mr. Herbert downstairs with him.

"The swan has been killed. I'll not have a threat like that in my parkland. I feel guilty, for my aunt and sister had both warned me about the bird, and I thought they overreacted. I ought to have done something before now."

The assurance from the rector was generous and forgiving, far more so than Hugh thought he deserved.

Some time later the apothecary sought them out in the library. "She needs quiet. That was a terrible shock. I've bled her and she is resting well now. But such an agitation of the nerves requires utter calm. Your aunt assures me that Miss Herbert will be given the best of care and rest here. Not," and he bowed to the Reverend Mr. Herbert, "that she could not recover at home, but I think it harmful to move her until tomorrow. She is very weak."

"She is welcome to remain here as long as necessary," Hugh said with no small degree of satisfaction. "She is well loved by my entire household."

"Good. Good." The apothecary said his farewells and departed, leaving Hugh and the rector in concerned silence.

"I wonder if Lady Susan will be displeased at my daughter remaining here?" the reverend mused.

"I believe that I am still master of this house. And I am not married to Lady Susan yet."

Mr. Herbert studied Hugh, but said nothing. Shortly they began a discussion about the missing book. When Hugh offered his theory, they speculated on where it could have been hidden. Tea and all that went with it was brought, with Mrs. Herbert following Crowder.

She accepted a cup of tea from Crowder, gracefully sitting on one of the leather chairs by the fireplace. "She was drifting off to sleep when I left her. I believe Mr. Herbert and I will return home. Perhaps we may come in the morning? I shall worry about her."

"Please—stay for dinner. You will feel easier if you see her this evening before you retire." Hugh knew he would have to as well, or he'd not sleep a wink.

So it was agreed that the Herberts would join the family for a quiet dinner.

Later, following a somber meal and a final visit with their daughter, they left. Elizabeth and Aunt Harriet sat with Tabitha for a bit before they headed for bed after a frantic and tiring day.

Hugh remained alone, George having deserted him as well. Even Septimus had crept back into Tabitha's room when no one was looking.

When he could stand it no longer, Hugh went up the stairs to the blue bedroom, paused to listen, then cracked the door open. There wasn't a sound from his darling girl. That she wasn't his made little difference. She would be.

He opened the door a little more to see Tabitha shifting restlessly on the vast bed. He went to her side. "Is there anything you wish? Can we do anything for you?"

"I do well enough. That fool bled me. I am not ill, just weak. I shall be as right as a trivet tomorrow."

"You will remain in bed until you are fit again." He knew the relief of her agreement before he left.

* * *

Lady Susan arrived early the following morning. "And how is your guest, Hugh, dear?" she asked sweetly.

"Fragile, I fear," Hugh replied, suspecting he exaggerated, but thinking it might serve his purpose.

"What did the apothecary say?"

"She is not to be moved until recovered."

"Really?" Lady Susan looked anything but pleased. "I should think she would want to go home."

"She will remain here until fit to leave."

Lady Susan was more than displeased, her eyes flashed with fury. "Well!"

Hugh assumed what he hoped to be a resolute mien. "Surely you would not wish Miss Herbert to sink into a decline?"

"I wish Miss Herbert . . ." Apparently Lady Susan thought better of her intended words, for she snapped her mouth closed.

"Quite so." Hugh nodded. "She will get the best of care. Here. And I trust you will have no objection."

Lady Susan absorbed the implacable expression on her betrothed's face and turned to depart. "I can see there is no chance of your pleasing me!"

Hugh made no effort to stop her, much to her obvious displeasure.

Chapter Twelve

Sir Anthony clattered down the stairs to join Hugh and Lady Susan in the entry. He glanced at Hugh, then the young lady standing near him and grinned. "Lady Susan, the sight of you is sufficient to brighten the gloomiest of days. I vow, you are lovelier each time I see you."

She bestowed a pleased smile on the baronet before casting a triumphant peek at her betrothed. "Just for that, you may have the delight of escorting me to Tonbridge. I wish to do a bit of shopping. Hugh says he won't go." She toyed with the furled parasol in her hands, fluttering her lashes and smiling in a most charming manner.

"Prettily said, dear lady," Tony replied with a bow. "It will be my pleasure. I'll fetch my hat and gloves and we can be on the way." When Lady Susan turned away at a sound from the library, Tony shrugged.

Hugh flashed Tony a quick smile. "I wish you a good day. There will be little enough to interest anyone around here—what with Miss Herbert requiring rest and quiet."

Tony ran up the stairs with a speed that would certainly please the young lady, any lady for that matter.

Hugh kept his eyes on his betrothed, who, seeing no more than a maid, had returned her attention to him.

"If she is so hardy, I should think she would pop out of bed first thing." Lady Susan gave Hugh a demure smile, but her eyes narrowed, challenging him.

"I wonder? What would you do if attacked by a forty-four pound bird, towed into the lake, and nearly drowned? The apothecary bled her and declared her in serious condition—her nerves." Hugh crossed his arms and regarded Lady Susan with stern eyes. There was a silence while she digested this shocking information.

"Oh. I did not realize she was in so frightful a state. I am sorry, Hugh. Give her my best wishes for a speedy recovery." She looked sincere.

"I am sure she will be happy to receive them. I wish you well with your shopping." Hugh turned to Tony when he rejoined them, gloves in hand, hat set on at a jaunty angle. Hugh's smile to his friend was the sort that wished him well in all things—notably a pursuit of the heiress.

Once the pair had left the house Hugh contemplated what to do next. Crowder closed the door behind him while Hugh stood mulling over his options. He walked to the library to find a book—something to appeal to an invalid.

What a complex business this was. He must behave in such a way that Susan cried off. Being bored was something she hated. He could do that. Indifference he might manage, too. She was pretty, no doubting that. If Tony or the quietly worthy Jasper could take charge of her, it would be splendid. Hugh would gracefully bow out with gratitude!

But there was the matter of Ainsworth. He strongly suspected that Tabitha didn't give two pins for the chap. It was necessary to convince her to dispose of her betrothed in such a manner that she didn't offend her family or the Ainsworths. *That* might prove to be a bit dicey. That Hugh intended to obtain marriage with the woman he truly loved was not a thing to be disputed. Just how!

Thoughts whirling about in his head, he left the library to go up the broad oak stairs. When he reached the blue bedroom he gently tapped on the door.

He entered when summoned, leaving the door ajar.

Tabitha was reclining against the pillows tucked behind her, looking slightly better than when he had checked on her earlier. "How are you feeling?"

"I should go home. I feel an utter fraud tucked up in this great bed with everyone fussing over me." She picked at the lace frill on the wristband of the pretty nightgown that Aunt Harriet insisted she wear. Her voice was not its usual strength. To Hugh's concerned eyes she looked wan.

"Nonsense. You are not to be moved. I'll not have it on my conscience that you had a relapse upon leaving here far too soon." He advanced to the foot of her bed to study her. Her silver gilt hair had been brushed into a shining fall about her pale face and her eyes appeared to reflect distress. "No, you'll stay where you are for the nonce."

With that satisfactory decision, he pulled up a chair after remembering to open the door a bit wider. "I have brought up a book from the library with the thought I might read to you. Would that be all right?"

Tabitha settled against her pillows with a sigh. "What luxury to have someone read to me. The book?"

"Something my aunt brought entitled *Emma*. Have you read it?" He held up the first volume of the book.

"I should like to hear you read to me." With more

pleasure than she would admit, she awaited the sound of his rich voice reading about sensible people. At one time she thought she liked the Gothic tales, but now found she preferred stories with true-to-life people.

The room was cozy. A gray mizzle now drifted down outside, but in here with the fire crackling merrily away and her covers pulled up to her chin, all was contentment.

Some time later Elizabeth poked her head around the door, then slipped inside, settling on the chaise longue while offering Tabitha a smile.

Tabitha wondered if Elizabeth was pleased with the intended marriage between her brother and Lady Susan. Elizabeth all too often punctured Lady Susan's superiority with her witty remarks, no indication of approval.

When a maid brought in a large tray bearing all that was needed for a lavish tea, Hugh put a slip of paper in the book to mark his place. "Ah, tea. My throat was beginning to think I'd never stop for refreshment."

"Now that is outrageous nonsense and you know it, brother dear," Elizabeth cried. "I must say that even though I've read the book, your reading of it certainly enhances the story." She beamed a smile at him.

Tabitha pushed herself up against the pillows. She had slid down while Hugh read, almost dozing off in spite of the excellent tale. Seeing her efforts her host quickly came to her aid, making certain she was comfortable.

"How good you are, Hugh. You shall make a fine husband." Elizabeth gazed at Tabitha, who blushed.

"You mean George does this for you?" He turned to give his sister a quizzical look.

"Naturally," Elizabeth replied. She wore a smug smile.

"So this is where everyone is!" Aunt Harriet declared. She entered the room to be followed by George and the maid with another well-laden tea tray.

"Oh, this is nice," Aunt Harriet said. She sighed in apparent contentment while George went over to sit by his wife, speaking softly to her for a minute or two.

"I see Tony took Lady Susan to Tonbridge so she might do some shopping. I am surprised she didn't insist that you take her." Aunt Harriet gave the baron a quizzical look.

He sipped his tea. Tabitha thought it seemed as though he was stalling, searching for an answer.

"Well, with Tabitha here I thought it rude to take off on a shopping expedition. Susan is not the easiest person to take visiting shops and buying who knows what. She must see everything." He exchanged a glance with George, who grinned in return.

Crowder appeared at the door, bowing stiffly to the baron. "Mr. Ainsworth is below, my lord. He has requested to see Miss Herbert. Shall I bring him up?" The portly butler inspected the pleasant scene as though he thought it a shame to spoil it by adding a stranger.

"Tabitha? Are we too much for you? Naturally you wish to see your betrothed." Hugh made as though to rise and Tabitha hastily motioned him to remain.

"I am sure that it would be far more proper to receive Mr. Ainsworth with all of you here instead of me—alone."

"How right you are, my dear," Aunt Harriet declared. Her white curls peeped out from under one of her splendid cambric-and-lace day caps and the warmth the fire and tea had given her rosy cheeks.

Tabitha fixed her gaze on the butler. "Bring Mr. Ainsworth upstairs, please, Crowder."

When Sam entered the blue bedroom it was plain to see the lavish room, the elegance of all the appointments, not to mention the assembled tea party, impressed him. "Good morning." Her voice wasn't strong, and she supposed she looked pale.

"I had not expected to find a room full of people after your ordeal." He seemed affronted and Tabitha failed to see why. Abominable creature, he had not one word of concern for her. He scarce came and she wished him gone.

"I am improving by the hour. They," and she waved her hand at the assembled group, "have been so kind as to keep me company for a brief time, just for tea, you know. Lord Latham has been reading to me," she added with the hope of provoking Sam. It failed to accomplish anything other than a puzzled expression on his face. According to Sam, only scholars and bluestockings read books—unless they were volumes on horse breeding.

"Mr. Ainsworth, please sit down over here and join us in tea," Aunt Harriet insisted. That the chair she gestured to was some distance from his betrothed apparently didn't occur to the lady. She signaled Crowder for more tea.

Sam obeyed at once. Familiar with tea customs in his own home, he soon made himself at ease, teacup in hand.

After a silence broken only by the clink of teaspoons on china, George ventured a remark on the weather. Elizabeth added her own comment. Hugh made a query regarding Sam's latest acquisition and all settled down to enjoy more tea. Aunt Harriet did the honors with the tea tray, seeing to it that no cup went empty. Tabitha put her spoon in her cup to signal she'd had all she wished. She settled back against

her pillow slightly fatigued, yet not wishing them to
go away. Her eyes drifted shut, but she paid attention
to what was being said.

Sam waxed eloquent on his latest horse. Hugh and
George nodded and listened with polite expressions.
She raised one lid to take note.

They consumed vast quantities of tea and demol-
ished most of the little treats on the serving plates.

Tabitha was about half-asleep with the drone of
voices. But in the back of her mind her dilemma refused to go away. How was she to dispense with her
engagement? She could not imagine marrying this
man who hadn't even so much as inquired how she
did. What an odious person he was, to be sure! She
really needed to study those young women at church.
There must be someone who would do!

Sam would be the squire eventually. And his
mother couldn't live forever. She racked her brain.
Surely there was some woman she had missed?

At long last, still without inquiring about her health
or expressing the least concern, Sam took his leave.
He'd made little effort to speak with her. He hadn't
brought her so much as a posy. He was a poor example of an engaged man. She doubted the baron would
behave like that.

The others left, and soon there were only Tabitha
and the baron remaining. Aunt Harriet had made a
point of seeing the door was well open when she went.
Tabitha smiled at that. How careful they were of the
proprieties.

She turned her gaze to the baron. He made a handsome picture with the gray sky behind him and the
fire flickering to one side in the hearth. Her heart sank
at the thought that he would soon belong to another.
She would never have the delight of running her fingers through his dark hair, or knowing his touch. Per-

haps one of her sisters might find a place for her? Should he actually wed Lady Susan, Tabitha wanted to be far away from Latham Court.

He tended to be serious, which was the first trait that had drawn her to him. She had never liked frivolous gentlemen. Sir Anthony was not precisely a fribble, but he took life casually. What a pity he wasn't paired with Lady Susan. Or perhaps the ever-faithful Jasper West?

She suddenly recalled the theft. "The manuscript!"

"There is time enough to search when you are better."

Tabitha considered the gravity of his expression, deciding it would be best to drop the subject for the moment.

Hugh began to read, only stopping when he observed that Tabitha had fallen into a much-needed sleep.

He stayed where he was, turning to stare into the crackling fire. He was no closer to a scheme whereby Lady Susan tossed him over for someone else. He would have to work more diligently at it. There would be no outings with her. He would take a page from Ainsworth and prose on and on about something she found boring. All flattery would cease, nor would he inquire about her health. Indeed, the worthy Mr. Ainsworth would merit study. All that he did around Tabitha would require emulating! For Lady Susan.

How could someone as sensitive as Tabitha tolerate the fellow? Or could she? Thinking back, Hugh hadn't noticed any blush on her cheeks when Sam came. Rather, she looked very annoyed at the dull Mr. Ainsworth and his talk of nothing but his new horse.

Hugh wondered how *he* might natter on to annoy Lady Susan. Shouldn't be too hard to think of something tedious.

Books! She found books irritating. She had been quite annoyed when he spent all that time with the translating. He might prose on about his books. When she and Jasper dropped in to call, as they seemed to do with increasing frequency, he could extol some very old and somber tome he was sure could be found on a library shelf. With a fond look at his little love, he tiptoed from the room, gently shutting the door behind him.

Not one to postpone things, Hugh slipped down to the library to inspect the various shelves. Within a short time he assembled the dullest collection ever seen. In fact, he wondered what possessed Lord Ingoldby to buy them in the first place.

Tony returned not long after that. Hugh listened to his old friend wax enthusiastic about the many charms of Lady Susan. Not the least of these, Hugh suspected, was the sizable estate and considerable dowry that accompanied the young lady when she married.

The following days found Hugh amusing Tabitha Herbert, especially when Lady Susan and Jasper might call.

Susan didn't become upset because Hugh didn't fuss over her, but she was irritated when Crowder announced that his lordship was occupied and could not be disturbed. When she at long last found him downstairs, Hugh eagerly invited her into the library. "You must see this book I found."

Susan reluctantly followed him. "Whatever now?" Jasper trailed behind them, looking mildly curious.

Hugh caught the lack of interest in her voice with rising hope. "Here." It was a treatise on Rome, comparing its government with that of Egypt. It could have been absorbing, but the writer had squeezed all life from the topic. Hugh began to read. Aloud. But not for long.

"Hugh—I truly do not care for that book." She interrupted him without an apology.

"But Lady Susan, it is a marvelous study. Miss Herbert thinks it vastly educational."

"Then read it to Miss Herbert," she snapped.

Hugh repressed a smile before picking up the next book on the pile he had assembled. "Surely you must admit this worthy of study. It is what has to be the ultimate examination of the works of Horace." He had scanned this and found that even he would have fallen asleep over its pages. It was as dull as ditchwater. "Listen." He proceeded to read from the introduction, which in itself was sufficient to put one into a stupor.

"Are you not going to tell me how ravishing I look in my new bonnet?" she demanded. She sounded goaded.

Hugh glanced up from the book to give what he hoped was a blank stare at her. "Bonnet? Oh, quite nice."

"Nice? I spent a small fortune on this and all you can say is that it is 'nice'?" She stamped her foot.

"Bad show," Jasper said in an aside. "Should always pay attention to bonnets."

"When there is so much to read, why would I be interested in mere bonnets?" Hugh gave Susan a bland look before returning to the book about Horace. "Now this," and he thumped the book, "is fascinating. I hope you know that I enjoy reading and spend hours and hours in my library. I would expect you to join me. Surely you wish to learn?"

"What I wish is . . ." She halted in midsentence and Hugh wondered what had stopped her. The most peculiar expression had come over her face, as though she recalled something. He wondered if her father had sent her over here with the injunction that she set a date for the wedding.

Tony breezed into the room, then paused as he saw the taut figures by the library desk.

"Sir Anthony, what do you think?"

"That has to be the most attractive bonnet I have seen in ages. Most becoming, my dear lady."

Drawing herself to her full height, Lady Susan wafted to his side, clinging to his arm. "Perhaps we might take a stroll by the lake? The sun has come out and I have no desire to stay in the house. All Lord Latham wants to do is sit here and read fusty old books. That is not for me!"

They left at once. Jasper paused by the door to give Hugh a quizzical look. "I don't know what your scheme is, but I suspect you are doing very well at it."

Hugh waited until Jasper had disappeared and chuckled.

The following days found him either with the dry-as-dust tomes or with Tabitha Herbert. Lady Susan looked ready to explode with exasperation. Tony grinned with enjoyment of the situation he obviously found to his liking.

In her room, Tabitha relished the hours that Lord Latham shared with her. He read from *Emma*, discussed some of his favorite books, or they simply talked. She was pleased they liked so many of the same things.

When he chanced to pass her open door and caught sight of her attempting to make her way from her bed to the chaise longue, he was horrified. He strode into the room, scooped her up into his arms, and ever so gently lowered her to the couch. "What do you think you are doing."

Tabitha thought he sounded furious. "Well, I cannot remain in that bed forever. I shall become too weak.

Allow me to be up and around. I have observed that the sooner people are active, the sooner they mend."

He clamped his mouth shut at her bit of wisdom. "If you become the least tired, you are to ring this bell and I will come at once to put you back in your bed." He handed her a small silver bell, which she set beside her. It didn't prevent her from attempting to walk again. When she knew he had gone from the house, she practiced.

She couldn't remain. It had been bad enough when she worked in the library. But to have him here, reading to her, discussing common interests, was far too entrancing. She had to leave!

Sam came again, finding her reclining on the chaise longue with a novel that Elizabeth had lent her.

"Well, at least you do not have a room full of people this time." He gave her a hostile look. "You are reading."

"If you must know, I adore reading. Don't you? I believe every *fine* gentleman should enjoy reading now and again." She stared at him with solemn eyes.

Sam looked uncomfortable.

"Why have you come?"

"Mother thinks it highly improper for you to remain here when you ought to have gone home."

"Tell your mother I shall leave when permitted by the apothecary. Lord Latham does not wish my health to be endangered." She primly folded her hands over the novel.

Again, Sam had not brought her so much as a limp petunia, nor had he uttered one word of sympathy.

She gestured to the bouquets of flowers set here and there in the room. "Lord Latham is so kind as to lavish these blooms on me. Lady Harriet sees to my every comfort. Dear Lady Purcell finds books for me to read—improving books, you may be sure." That was a stretch of the truth, but they did improve Tabitha's frame of mind. "I am not eager to return home."

"I hope you do not intend to be a languishing sort of female once we wed." He scowled at her.

Tabitha repressed a strong desire to shudder. The sooner she could get to church to find another girl, the better it would be.

"I might. One never knows. Since your mother is so capable, I may just let her run the house and everything. I would be able to read to my heart's content." Tabitha beamed a beatific smile at him.

Sam was not happy with her reply. She could see that he expected far more. He sputtered his disagreement with this heresy. "Mother will not approve!" He stomped from the room, not noticing that Tabitha failed to bid him farewell.

She stared out of the window, wondering what she could say that would send Sam fleeing in search of another.

"I heard Ainsworth before he left, Tabitha," the baron said from the doorway. "He did not exactly lower his voice." He lounged against the frame of the door. "I warned you about living with his mother."

"I am aware of the difficulties." Tabitha firmed her resolve to send Sam into the arms of another woman.

The baron remained where he was, yet Tabitha felt the pull of his attraction from where she reclined. This was a dangerous situation, to be near him and yet so restricted.

"Tomorrow I shall get up and dress," she declared in a resolute manner. She flashed him a defiant look, daring him to object. "I shall walk about the house and perhaps I can find the missing book."

He merely raised a brow as though he defied her to do so.

Chapter Thirteen

The very next day Tabitha left her bed as soon as she felt able. With the help of a maid she dressed in the washed and pressed gown she had worn the day of the attack. Just to have her clothes on again perked her up. She managed the walk to the chaise longue without falling flat on her face. Things were definitely encouraging.

She ate the contents of the tray brought up from the kitchen though she had little appetite. How could she expect to find the book if she didn't have the energy?

She was determined to locate it. All she had to do was to think like Lady Susan, for Tabitha was quite sure that young lady had hidden the valuable book in some nook. How Lord Latham would regard such a discovery she preferred not to consider. It was hateful enough to know he could not be hers, let alone imagine how he might view his affianced lady being exposed by Tabitha Herbert! Her comfort was that Lady Susan was not likely to take on the work of copyist!

After learning that the baron had left on some errands, she decided she would make her search at once. The upper floor was quiet. The upstairs maids were occupied in making beds and dusting rooms. She decided that if her suspicions were correct Lady Susan could not have had the time to go upstairs, find a good hiding place, then back down to the drawing room. She would have needed more time for that. No, in order to locate that book Tabitha must search the main floor again. There had to be a spot that was available, yet unobtrusive—but where?

Her legs trembled as she made her way to the main floor of the house. Tottering into the library, she plopped down in one of the leather chairs while considering the matter. Every cabinet, every shelf in here had been gone through. Nothing had been found.

In the anteroom she did the same.

Finding the entry hall vacant, she walked around to the dining room door. Where would one go after leaving here? She tried to recall precisely what direction Lady Susan had taken. In the hall, she sank down on a straight, hard chair conveniently close. There were a number of these chairs, lined up against the walls like so many mahogany soldiers. They were not comfortable, but at the moment she was more concerned about not falling on her face.

"Think!" she muttered. That dratted book simply did *not* vanish into thin air. Wherever it was concealed *had* to be a place large enough to hide it.

Discouraged, she made her way to the stairway and plunked herself down, too tired to walk up to the blue bedroom where she had been living the past few days.

Crowder found her sitting on the second step from the bottom, leaning against the beautifully carved oak banister. She longed for a cup of tea. She gave the portly butler a resigned look. He would probably scold her.

"Miss Herbert!" He looked and sounded totally aghast.

"I cannot remain in bed forever, Crowder. I believe that if I have a cup of tea I will be quite all right."

Crowder turned aside to speak to someone, then gave Tabitha a reproving look. "Tea will be here shortly."

Tabitha smiled. An unorthodox place to have tea— on the second to the bottom step. "Thank you." She paused to think a few moments before asking, "Crowder, we have looked so many places for that missing book. Is there a cupboard few are aware of, where a book might be hidden?"

The tea tray arrived with a curious maid whom Crowder immediately sent on her way. He placed the nicely laden tray on a distinctive marble-topped table.

Tabitha watched him as he poured tea into a delicate china cup while pondering her question. "There is a concealed cupboard beneath this stairs, Miss Herbert. No one has used it in years. Indeed, I quite forgot it was there. It is not needed, you see."

Ignoring the proffered teacup, Tabitha rose to her feet. "Where?" she demanded urgently. "Oh, tell me where it is. It is possible that whoever took the book stashed it there for a later retrieval."

The butler frowned a few moments. After replacing the teacup, he walked to the side of the grand staircase to study the oak paneling. Then he nodded, walked to a panel to touch a bit of carving. The panel swung open.

Tabitha, who had followed hard on Crowder's heels, knelt down to peer inside the dim interior.

"I do believe the book is here! Look, Crowder! How odd that no one recalled this storage place." She gently removed the book, clasped it to her, then slowly rose to her feet. She was trembling again, but with excitement.

"As to that, it simply has not been used as far back as I can remember. There is nothing else in there. The house does not lack for storage areas, you see."

"How clever of you to think of it now." Tabitha studied the book to discover if anything in it had been damaged in the hasty snatch. If her theory were correct, Lady Susan would have had to dash to the library, grab the book, rush to the hiding place to stow the book before the men left the dining room. She had entered the drawing room in a subdued manner, and had been away just long enough to give the impression that she had been to the water closet.

"This is somewhat concealed from the dining room door, is it not? Definitely," she answered herself as she checked. "How many people knew of this hiding place?"

The butler rubbed his chin while he considered the question. "It was never what you might call a secret. I should imagine that a number of people knew."

Tabitha set the book on the step before joining it. She truly needed her cup of tea now.

Crowder seemed to read her mind for he proffered the cooling tea. Tabitha consumed it with unladylike gulps. The butler didn't raise a one of his wispy brows, but poured a second cup when she held out the empty teacup. Tabitha sipped her tea. Rising disquiet began to flow through her.

"His lordship will be greatly pleased, miss."

"Yes, I expect he will," she replied absently, deep in thought. Just what *would* his reaction be? Would he leap to defend his betrothed if Tabitha revealed her suspicions? "Crowder, would you carry the book to the library for me? I shall manage with the teacup." At least she thought she could. Although it seemed her strength was improving. That just proved what solving a mystery did for one.

The butler did as asked, a pleased smile on his face as he placed the book on the vast desk at the far end of the room. "There you are, miss. When he returns I will tell his lordship that you are here with a surprise, shall I?" Both the wispy brows shot up.

"Perfect. I will rest here and need not bother going to my room." She sank into the comfort of a large leather chair and finished her tea. She could leave with the mystery solved. She didn't know if she could go on assisting him. It was difficult to be near him and feel as she did. She had never supposed that wanting someone, loving someone could be so fraught with pain.

She was about half asleep when Lord Latham entered the library, his steps brisk and purposeful. Sir Anthony sauntered in behind him looking curious.

"What is all this about a surprise? Crowder explained you had made your way down here just after I left the house. Are you mad?" He placed his hands on his trim hips and stared down his aristocratic nose at her.

"Not in the least." Tabitha gave him a justifiably smug smile. "Take a look on your desk." She watched while the baron strode to the other end of the room. She knew the moment he saw the book. He straightened, looked back at her, then to the book again.

"Where?" He glanced at his friend, then at her.

"Under the staircase. Crowder showed me the not-so-secret storage place. I vow you could put a fair number of things inside there. It is quite roomy."

"What made you think it might be there?" he accused.

Seeing that he was becoming just as suspicious as she had feared, Tabitha said, "I *didn't* know about it. I suspected a certain person and figured that if that person were to hide the book—for whatever reason—

it couldn't be far away from the drawing room and the dining room. I asked Crowder if there was a cupboard we had missed. He thought of the place under the stairs. That was it."

The baron looked rather formidable, much like the image of him she had carried when younger and spoke of him as the Black Baron. It had taken time for her to decide that he was not the villain they had believed.

Now, he looked incensed. "Who is your suspect?"

"You won't like it," she prophesied.

"Allow me to be the judge of that." He was definitely the haughty peer, generations of the bluest blood revealed in his face and pose.

"Lady Susan absented herself for a time right after we left the dining room. She could conceivably have taken the book, hidden it, and joined the other women in the drawing room before you gentlemen came in."

"I cannot believe Lady Susan capable of such behavior." He toyed with the polished seal that hung from his fob pocket. He crossed the room to stand before her, staring down at her, his eyes puzzled.

"It isn't the most intelligent thing to do, granted," Tabitha shot back, incensed that he would doubt her and yet understanding his reluctance to accuse his promised wife.

Sir Anthony cleared his throat as though to remind them he was still in the room. Tabitha was glad he was there to ease the tension.

Elizabeth whirled into the library as Tabitha and the baron stared at each other, mutual hostility tangible in the air like a gray cloud.

"Crowder said you found the book under the stairs!" Ignoring the frozen couple, she dashed to the desk to ascertain the truth for herself. "It *is* here. Marvelous! Now we can cease wondering if someone crept

into the house to make off with the valuable object."
She slowly joined them, looking from one to the other.
"Now what is the matter? You should be in alt to
have your precious book back."

"I told him he wouldn't like it," Tabitha grumbled.
"He insisted upon knowing who I suspected. I told
him. He did *not* like it at all when I said I believed
Lady Susan was the culprit." She shifted in the chair.

"He doubts Lady Susan had anything to do with it?
I suspected her all along. Well, I suppose love is blind,
only I have never thought of dearest Hugh in that
light. Usually he is awake on all suits." She turned to
her brother. "Hugh, darling, what is the problem?"

"*You* also think it is Susan?" He stared at his sister.

"Well, *I* didn't take it, nor did Aunt Harriet or
George. Sir Anthony wouldn't. Stands to reason the
rector and his wife wouldn't, nor would Tabitha. But
Susan practically grew up here. She would have re-
membered that out-of-sight spot. I cannot imagine
why that hiding place didn't occur to me. But—*why*
did she do it?" Elizabeth crossed her arms before her,
tapping her dainty foot, while giving her brother an
arch look.

"Elizabeth . . ."

The sound of voices in the hall brought all attention
to those arriving. Four faces turned to the doorway at
once. Two of them wore exceedingly cool expressions.

"Miss Herbert! You are well enough to be downstairs." Lady Susan strolled into the room casting a
complacent glance at Tabitha. Jasper West trailed
after her, as usual.

"I fancy you will be returning to your home now?"
Sir Anthony crossed his arms to study the lady while
he lounged against the fireplace mantel.

Lady Susan was garbed in the height of fashion, her

jonquil pelisse attractively contrasting with her dusky curls and dark eyes. She had such charm. She was also determined to have her own way.

Tabitha nodded her agreement with Lady Susan's assessment. Tabitha would shortly be leaving here.

"Crowder said you had received a surprise. I trust it was a good one?" Lady Susan glowed with a confident air, seeming assured as well as utterly beautiful.

Tabitha could see what the baron might find bewitching about her. Lady Susan intrigued and enchanted.

"The book has been found." The baron studied Lady Susan with a piercing gaze. "It was under the stairway."

There was no mistaking her start of surprise or her obvious disappointment in the discovery.

Tabitha thought Susan's recovery quite impressive.

"Found?" She was her charming self within a few seconds. "What a strange place to place it."

"True," the baron replied in a properly grave manner.

"Why would anyone put it there?" Lady Susan queried in a rather uneasy way. Her expression remained guileless.

Tabitha exchanged a look with Elizabeth. The clear summation offered on Lady Susan should have had an effect on his lordship. Yet, it was likely he wouldn't want to accuse her. Men were such fools about women. Notably women with dark flashing eyes and fetching brown curls.

"That is a question I should like answered," Lord Latham said in a velvety voice, one that sent shivers down Tabitha's spine. "Few people know about that cupboard. It hasn't been used in years."

"Well," Lady Susan said in a considering manner, "it isn't very convenient, is it?" Then she said coyly,

"I want you to take me to the next assembly, and perhaps on picnics and to parties. Now I suppose you will bury your nose in that dreary book again." She looked vastly annoyed, like a child deprived of a favorite toy.

"You knew of that hiding spot, for we hid there when we were children while playing at tag." He did as Elizabeth had done and crossed his arms before him. He looked overpowering—his tall, lean, and romantic figure so handsome, that patrician face so cold, so aloof. Had Tabitha not seen him smiling and laughing before, she would have been terrified. She waited to see what Lady Susan would do next.

"Well—so what if I concealed the book for a time? I fail to see why you are making such a fuss about it. You have the dratted book back now." She cast an insinuating look at Tabitha. "But I'll wager you might change your mind about having Miss Herbert as your copyist. I feel sure a more appropriate person could be found—a gentleman. I think it unseemly that she is here." She sidled up to him to place a slim hand on his arm. "You would do that to please me, would you not?"

"You believe Miss Herbert is a threat to you?"

"No, no," Lady Susan answered hastily. "I am merely concerned about the proprieties of the matter."

"Miss Herbert's father is our local rector. The library door remains open—anyone could walk in here at any time. I have found Miss Herbert a splendid copyist. I see no reason to replace her." To Tabitha he added, "I expect you will want some time at home to regain your usual calm. Once you do, please return. I shall endeavor to have a stack of pages for you to write out in your meticulous hand."

Tabitha let out the breath she hadn't realized she

was holding. How bittersweet—to remain working in here with him as she longed to do when he would be as remote as though he were on the moon.

"Very well," she replied in a meek little voice. After all, it was better than not seeing him entirely.

Elizabeth threw up her hands and murmured something about seeing Aunt Harriet. Lady Susan persuaded Lord Latham to show her something in the picture gallery. Sir Anthony strolled after, muttering something about his room.

Tabitha didn't care a jot. Well, she did, but little good it did her. She waited for Jasper to leave as he usually did, following Lady Susan like a shadow.

"Miss Herbert, it would seem you are the heroine of the hour. I must congratulate you. It would seem Hugh isn't going to scold Susan." He examined her with shrewd eyes.

"It would appear his lordship is so thankful to have the book returned that he isn't going to pursue the matter. I can understand that, since she is his betrothed."

"Yet, you are not pleased about it?"

"Why? I doubt *you* will do anything about her." She shifted uneasily as he paced back and forth near her. She didn't know why, but he made her wary.

He glanced at her from moment to moment. "Come, let us examine the book to make certain nothing is missing."

Before Tabitha could protest, he had grabbed one of her hands to pull her to her feet, then nudged her in the direction of the baron's desk. "Sir, I protest. You know nothing of this book or what condition it was in before."

"But you do." He gestured to the book, centered on the top of the fine mahogany desk.

Her feeling of unease sent prickles of discomfiture

through her. "Why are you doing this?" She tried to free herself from his grasp and failed.

"I must confess I enjoy being with you. This is a means to have you away from others and to myself."

"Anyone could walk in here at any moment. I fail to see why . . ." Her words were cut off when Jasper grabbed her to his chest. He proceeded to kiss her— in a rough and quite objectionable manner. She managed to turn her head to one side and tried to push him away.

The baron and Lady Susan chose that moment to return.

"Oh, dear," tittered Lady Susan. "Jasper is such an impetuous man. But then, some men do like blondes."

Tabitha managed to wrest free from Jasper's hold. "It isn't what you think . . ." she began.

"It is very obvious to me, Miss Herbert." The baron's words were clipped and cold. He looked as though she had played him false.

"Well, it shouldn't be." Tabitha took a step from the odious Mr. West. "He claimed he wanted to see the book, to check if there was damage, although what he'd know about that is more than I can see. Then he grabbed me and pulled me over to the desk." She bestowed a withering look on her assailant. "Sir, I find your assault quite revolting." Unfortunately, he didn't wither easily. He merely appeared amused at her protestation. She longed to punch him.

"I suppose that is one way to view it," Lady Susan said, sounding far too gleeful.

"Oh, dear, do I interrupt something interesting?" Aunt Harriet babbled as she trotted into the room. "I heard the book had been recovered and wanted to see it for myself. How clever of you, my dear, to think it might be hidden close by the dining room. Crowder is so proud of himself. I suppose you must take a day off to compose yourself, but you will return to be Hugh's copyist shortly, won't you?"

She bustled to the desk while she spoke, separating Tabitha from Jasper with an efficient sweep of one arm. One look at Tabitha's face and she quietly added, "My dear girl—you look too pale. I insist you come with me. What you need now is a little rest. Now." Aunt Harriet prodded Tabitha ahead of her until they had left the library and Jasper West and his odd behavior behind them.

Lady Susan could be heard exclaiming about the interrupted scene as she and the baron followed. Tabitha wished she could convince the baron of her innocence. At the moment he didn't seem in the least reasonable.

"I take it you were in the process of pushing that scheming man away from you?" Aunt Harriet spoke softly.

"I was." Tabitha was thankful for her discretion. Why Mr. West attacked her was beyond understanding. She could see why it was deemed advisable for a young lady to have someone present when she was with a gentleman. Not all of them behaved as they ought, obviously.

"Where are you bound, Aunt Harriet?" The baron paused in the entry to pin his aunt with his gaze. Lady Susan clung to his arm, looking pleased.

Aunt Harriet gave a slight sniff. "I believe it best for Tabitha to rest. Mr. West's onslaught was enough to send a less resolute girl into the vapors. She requires tranquility. I intend to see she gets it." She fixed her nephew with the sort of look that he knew boded ill.

Hugh watched his aunt and Tabitha make their way up the stairs. They conversed quietly. He had no idea what was said, but he suspected his aunt wanted to know what had occurred. As to why, it was completely beyond him. As far as he could recall Jasper West had never so much as looked twice at Tabitha in the past. Why, of a sudden, would he attack her now? And why was Susan so gleeful about it?

It had hit Hugh hard when he had walked into the library to see Tabitha in West's arms. He admitted he wanted her in *his* arms, not anyone else's. He gazed at Lady Susan with thoughtful eyes. Why had she not been more surprised? It would bear consideration.

"Well, since your copyist is under the weather yet, I see no reason why you cannot take me to the assembly at Tonbridge. I have a pretty new dress I am dying to wear."

"You ought to know by now that I am unwilling to take in an assembly. Not even to please you. Understand that once we are wed I will not be dragged all over creation to attend assemblies or card parties, much less shopping. I have more important things to do." He peered down at her with hopeful eyes. He detected a tightening of her mouth.

"I suppose I shall have to beg Sir Anthony to take me." She stepped from Hugh's side with a flounce.

"You may try, of course," he said with a bow.

"Otherwise, Jasper will do the pretty. He is always so thoughtful of me."

Hugh decided she didn't seem terribly disappointed that he refused to escort her. Her cousin Jasper would do admirably.

Now, all that was required was that he convince the two of them to make it a permanent arrangement.

Chapter Fourteen

"So, what are you going to do about Susan's bit of spite?" Tony asked. "Let it pass? I doubt she's the least sorry for her behavior." Tony lounged back in his chair, savoring the fine brandy from his host's cellar. He studied Hugh from over the rim of his glass. "Was your betrothal one of those things understood within the family for years? That is too often the case. She's beautiful—but a widget."

"Her father spoke of it often as we were growing up. I thought it might serve. And I doubt it would do any good to chastise Lady Susan. She has her own ethics." Hugh glanced at his good friend, then contemplated the fire burning in the carved stone fireplace on this damp summer day when it felt more like April than June. "The more time I spend with Tabitha Herbert, the more I realize that I have far more interest in her than I do in Lady Susan. I suspect that she, on the other hand, begins to think me utterly boring. At least, I hope so." He grinned at Tony.

Tony gave a shout of laughter. "Oh, my dear Hugh, if you could have heard her on the way to Tonbridge. She waxed on and on about her fears of her life with you. Had I any sympathy for you at all, I should whisk her off to Gretna Green and remove her from your hands."

Hugh returned his gaze to Tony. "Well?"

Tony inhaled sharply. "As much as I like the chit, I cannot see myself spending the next forty or so years with her. I don't doubt that if we should have children, they would be relegated to the nursery whilst she waltzed off to London for the Season and a chance to display her beauty."

"One cannot deny that beauty, though. Without a doubt she would produce lovely offspring."

"With the same empty heads?" Tony shook his.

"What about Jasper? She seems to depend on him. Wherever one is, the other is sure to be. He is like her shadow." Hugh stared at the fine amber liquid in his glass before darting a glance at Tony.

"Ah, the lad who took liberties with Miss Tabitha?" Tony sipped his brandy while considering the matter.

"There obviously is a strong liking between Lady Susan and Jasper—perhaps more than that? It would be a happy thing if he chanced to inherit from the uncle she mentioned—the one he is named after who has pots of money. The earl would be spared another Season in London. West might even be able to secure a title should he desire—given ample money."

"Indeed," Tony replied absently, then gave his friend a grin. "I am off tomorrow. This morning Crowder gave me a letter from my mother. Seems she wants me for something."

"I shall miss you." Hugh frowned into the fire. Things wouldn't be the same with Tony gone.

"But—think on it. Without me around—and you with your nose in that book, Lady Susan *must* rely on her cousin to escort her. Or can you hold out against her charms? You will be required to spend more time with the fetching Miss Herbert. Poor lad. I truly pity you."

"Tabitha is easy on the eyes, isn't she?" Hugh replied with a dry smile. "Her hair is most unusual—silver gilt."

"Intelligent conversation, as well. Hugh—I hope everything turns out the best for you. That you are able to tempt Lady Susan to break your engagement. Then you will be free to do as you wish."

"You are optimistic, my friend. You assume Miss Herbert will fall into my arms like a ripe plum."

"I have seen her watch you. In my estimation the girl is in love with you, whether she knows it or not. I doubt you will have any problems."

"Except Sam Ainsworth!" Hugh reminded.

"Egad! I had completely forgotten about the worthy clod. I refuse to believe that Miss Herbert cares two pins for that chap. Do not give up hope yet. She'll withdraw."

"Thank you—I think." Having finished their brandy, the two men went to the desk to take another look at the priceless book that had been hidden under the stairs.

Tabitha had been home for a day before her mother inquired about Sam Ainsworth and what Tabitha planned.

"I don't know. I was a fool to accept him. Oh, Mama, I cannot marry him! We would have to live with his parents! That might not be so ill except his mother . . ."

"It would create problems were you to cry off."

"I had thought," Tabitha confided, "to find a girl who would suit Sam Ainsworth far better than I would. *We* would be at daggers drawn in no time at all."

"Mary Ann Gower returned from a visit to her relatives up north while you were recovering at the Court," Mrs. Herbert said casually. "I saw her eyeing Sam Ainsworth last Sunday at church. Is there a way we might ever so chance to put her in his way? I believe she adores horses and dogs."

"Mama, what a love you are!" Tabitha hugged her mother with more than a little gratitude. "I realized I would far rather be a spinster the rest of my life than marry him. But will Mrs. Ainsworth approve of Mary Ann?"

"I might drop a word or two in her ear about the sweet, docile nature of the girl, as well as her excellent dowry." Mrs. Herbert cast an amused look at her daughter.

The very next day Tabitha happened to see Mary Ann Gower at the village shop. She was buying sweetmeats.

"Miss Herbert! I heard about your frightful accident. I trust you are well recovered?" The girl had a pleasant voice, was neatly garbed, and her manners would surely meet Mrs. Ainsworth's exacting standards.

"I am fine, thank you." Tabitha noted Mary Ann lingered as though she wished to talk.

They left the shop and strolled along the walk together. "You had an agreeable visit in the north?"

"Yes. I was surprised to learn that you had become engaged to Mr. Ainsworth. I never dreamt the two of you would suit. *You* do not ride and *he* prizes his horses."

"Well, there *are* problems. I like to read and he does not. As you say, he dotes on horses and dogs and I feel lukewarm about them. I fear I shall never agree with Mrs. Ainsworth on anything. I cannot deny I have a few doubts." Normally Tabitha would *not* have been so confiding to one she didn't know well, but she had a motive—to plant a few seeds in Mary Ann's mind and hope for the best.

"What a pity. My cousin raises foxhounds. I adore dogs. They live in good hunting country. 'Tis a shame you don't ride. Most country girls do. I enjoy it ever so much. But then, you don't have a horse, so you?" She thought a few moments, then said, "What caused your accident?"

"Well, a swan attacked me. It was quite horrid." She was about to offer details when she saw Sam riding into the village on one of his prize mares. She waved at him.

Mary Ann seemed perfect for Sam. If she could just interest Sam in the pretty Mary Ann, with her chestnut curls and pleasing gray eyes, it would answer her problem. The girl loved dogs and horses and didn't sound bookish.

He promptly rode to where she stood with Mary Ann. He looked splendid on his horse. A side-glance revealed all Tabitha hoped for. Mary Ann Gower was top over toes in love with the estimable Sam.

"Mr. Ainsworth, I believe you know Miss Mary Ann Gower? She has just returned from visiting her cousin. They breed hunting dogs and ride to the hounds. Is that not so, Miss Gower?" Tabitha beamed a bright smile at Mary Ann, hoping that she would not be shy.

"Do they now?" Sam swung down from his horse to offer Mary Ann a polite bow. "What sort does your cousin have?"

Tabitha's ears were numbed with a catalog of the breed of hounds and the lineage of the horses the cousin raised. Sam was clearly impressed. He almost drooled at the image of those dogs and horses Mary Ann listed.

With a murmured excuse, Tabitha slipped back into the shop. She doubted the pair noticed that she had gone. At last, Sam must have recalled his errand for he bowed again, said a few words in parting, then remounted and rode toward the blacksmith shop farther down the road.

Tabitha whirled from the village shop to rejoin Mary Ann. "Sorry, I forgot something my mother wanted. Did you have an agreeable talk with Mr. Ainsworth?"

"Yes, indeed I did." She didn't add to that, but her expression was bemused, as though she had received a gift she hadn't expected.

At the rectory gate Tabitha parted from Mary Ann with a feeling that great strides forward had been made in Tabitha's plan to bestow Sam on someone else.

Her mother at once wanted to know all that occurred in the village. Both were satisfied with her progress. Not that they expected instant success, but it was a beginning.

Lady Susan, with the inevitable Jasper West at her heels, strolled into Latham Court as though she were already its mistress.

Crowder gave her his stiffest bow, then marched off to the library to announce that guests had arrived.

"I take it you are not pleased with the arrivals?" Hugh inquired quietly of his faithful butler.

"It is not for me to disapprove of callers, my lord."

Hugh grinned at the lofty tone of his reply. Whoever had come, it was someone Crowder disliked. A rustle of silk in the adjacent room gave a hint.

Susan entered the room with her skirts flowing about her. She reminded him of a ship entering a harbor at full sail. She looked vexed, as did Jasper West.

"La, Hugh, do tell Crowder he needn't announce *us*. We are like family." She walked up to his desk where Hugh had taken refuge when he suspected who had come to call.

"Crowder knows that when I am at work, I dislike being disturbed." Hugh rose from his chair with obvious reluctance, something she noticed at once.

"I thought that with Miss Herbert away you would be free to do things." She flashed an annoyed look at him. "This is as bad as when you were translating the book and she served as copyist. You are *not* fun. In fact, you border on being boring, dearest Hugh. You must mend your ways!"

"I suppose you want to do something. The weather is rather inclement today—or is it next week you want?"

"An assembly is coming up. I should like to go. And I expect *you* to take me there." She said the words much like she was throwing down a gauntlet.

"I do believe I told you that I do not as a rule attend assemblies." Hugh saw his error when her eyes lit up. He should have flatly stated he had no intention of going to this assembly or anything else she wanted to do.

"You can go this time. I insist. People will speculate if we are not seen out and about together once in a while."

"Perhaps we can get up a party? I imagine Elizabeth and George would like to go. Perhaps Miss Herbert and Mr. Ainsworth as well?" He refused to be alone with her.

Lady Susan compressed her lips and looked about to stamp her feet to get her way when her cousin nudged her arm. At once she simmered down, like a kettle removed from a fire. "Very well. We can all go together."

"We will bring the barouche," Jasper offered.

"And I will have ours. Perhaps there is another young lady we can include? I'll ask Elizabeth."

That he would ask his sister and not her didn't appear to annoy Lady Susan. She seemed satisfied that she had managed to get her own way at long last.

They departed not long after. Elizabeth entered the library once the earl's curricle had left.

"Can you think of a young lady to augment our party this coming Saturday? You and George are joining Susan and me, along with Jasper, of course, at the next assembly."

"Never say you gave in to her demands? But you did, otherwise you wouldn't ask about another girl for Jasper. I will check with Tabitha. She will know of someone useful."

Hugh laughed. "Do you have any notion of how that sounded, sister dear? Useful for what?"

"Why," she gave him a virtuous look, "for scheming. I fully intend to hunt for another girl for Mr. Ainsworth!"

The following Saturday the party set off early for Tonbridge. Included was the very delighted Mary Ann Gower.

Elizabeth queried the choice, but Tabitha firmly replied that she had her reasons. Elizabeth, detecting a plot afoot, beamed in response.

When the carriages set forth for Tonbridge, somehow Sam ended up sitting by the pretty Mary Ann while Tabitha perched next to Jasper West, maintaining a cautious distance. She didn't trust him in the slightest.

It was a pity that attending this assembly meant so little to Tabitha for she had always relished them. Other than the hope she nurtured of throwing Mary

Ann at Sam's head, she had little expectation of enjoying the evening.

The assembly proved to be especially fine. An excellent musical group performed the succession of dances with perfect harmony and splendid tempo.

Tabitha, garbed in a simple white muslin embellished with rows of exquisite lace her sister Nympha had sent her, knew she looked well enough. With Jasper occupied watching his cousin Susan, Tabitha had a chance to observe the growing attachment between Sam Ainsworth and Mary Ann Gower. Tabitha couldn't believe the flirting that the usually heedless Sam bestowed on a delighted Mary Ann. Actually, she was probably too good for Sam. However, if she were in love with the fellow, perhaps it would do well.

"Would you care to dance, Miss Herbert?" The rich tones of the baron's voice broke Tabitha's contemplation.

"Indeed, sir, I would." She quickly rose, offering him her hand at once. They strolled along to join a set for a country dance. A favorite melody—"Kiss Me Sweetly"—soon floated out over the dancers. Tabitha had performed this dance many times, but this was different.

She had not danced with Lord Latham before. When they met in the center of the line she glanced up, her eyes meeting his. Could there be a message in those rich brown depths? It lasted but a moment or two and then they separated once again. But she took note that every time they met in the pattern of the dance, he held her eyes with his compelling gaze. She hadn't the faintest idea who else joined in the country dance. She only had eyes for him.

By the time the dance concluded, she felt breathless. It would be a memory to treasure. "I thank you, sir. That was lovely." What message he conveyed with his eyes she dare not trust. It seemed to her he sent a look of love.

The baron did not return her to where Elizabeth and George waited. "You appear angelic this evening," he said while they promenaded along the side of the dancers after the next dance began. "You are all white and pearl, with your hair an added celestial touch." He drew her close to his side. "I am glad the accident did no lasting harm."

She smiled at him. "I believe it was much harder on the swan."

He chuckled. "That was not an angelic reply, Miss Herbert. You ought to have had pity on the swan."

"Never. He received his proper end," was her pert reply. "I have no pity for the nasty creature."

"I understand he was much enjoyed by all." They walked a few steps in silence, absorbed in themselves and ignoring the good-humored throng of dancers.

"I am well enough to return to my copying, sir." Tabitha insisted, although not aggressively. She would only go to Latham Court if he truly wanted her to return.

"That would be very welcome. I fear you will be dismayed at the pile of paper awaiting your skills. I have not been idle, you see."

"I think it admirable that you pursue this task with such determination." Ahead of them she saw Mr. West near Elizabeth. He was rather unhappy if his petulant expression was a clue. She wished she might avoid him.

"Your next partner?" the baron asked. "You are very forbearing of his recent attack on you."

"It was *most* strange. It is a pity he could not dance every dance with Lady Susan," she murmured without considering the man to whom she spoke. "All he does is watch her—no matter who her partner is." Then

her ill-chosen words penetrated and she could feel the
heat of her blush rising. "Oh, I do beg your pardon.
I had no right to say that." She hoped she looked as
contrite as she felt. He made no reply. In fact, he
looked rather thoughtful.

The remainder of the evening went by faster than
she had expected. After the baron sought her out,
many other gentlemen requested her hand for a dance.
She did not sit out a one! But he did not seek her
hand again.

When it was time to depart it was the baron who
located her blue twilled sarsenet shawl. He placed it
about her shoulders with a gentle touch. "If you could
be at the Court on Monday morning, I would be
greatly in your debt."

She spun around to face him. "I will be there."

Sam stood near them. Tabitha noted that he paid
her not the slightest heed. If she had cared for him,
she would have been desolate. Tabitha rejoiced he was
deep in conversation with Mary Ann.

"Mr. Ainsworth seems rather taken with Miss
Gower," the baron observed.

"Yes, he does, doesn't he," Tabitha replied with all
the satisfaction of a schemer who is repaid for her
efforts. "She is the perfect match for him."

"You intend to break your betrothal with him?"

Tabitha gave the baron a guilty look. "Well . . ."

Lady Susan marched over to cling to the baron's
arm, preventing any words that might have been
voiced.

The two vehicles returned to Rustcombe blessed
with a full moon and tolerable roads. Only Lady Susan
chatted with enthusiasm about the assembly. All the
others appeared to be deeply in thought—for one reason or another.

*   *   *

The next morning Elizabeth found her brother seated at the breakfast table dawdling over a cup of coffee, the remains of a partly eaten meal before him.

"Well, dear brother. You will join us in church today?" At his nod, she continued. "Have you taxed Lady Susan regarding her hiding that valuable book?"

"No, but I wonder if it would accomplish a thing?" Hugh studied his sister. Her pregnancy agreed with her, she simply glowed with good health and happiness.

"She might be annoyed enough to decide you are not the husband for her. She does not like to be chastised—she never has. Remember as a child how she always had to have her way. I cannot see you marrying her and living a happy life. It is a pity you are such an honorable gentleman, else you could just tell her you doubt you would suit. It has been done. George was engaged to another before we met." At his start of surprise she nodded.

"I had no idea."

"No, it is scarcely a thing one proclaims. When we met he said he knew at once he could not marry her and he told her so. Fortunately, she was gracious about it. I suspect she had another interest so it worked well all around. There is nothing to prevent you from doing the same." She took a bite of her toast while giving her dearest brother a hopeful look.

"I shall do as you suggest—at least taxing her about her reasons for hiding the book. She sought attention."

"Well, she is as guilty as sin." Elizabeth poured herself another cup of tea and ate a hearty meal.

Lady Susan and Jasper stopped off at Latham Court on their way home from the church service.

While Hugh normally would have been dismayed,

for once he looked forward to the meeting. He hadn't been able to say a word following church. He had noticed that Sam Ainsworth was busy introducing Miss Gower to his mother. Did Tabitha actually plot such a romance? A quick study of her revealed nothing.

"Lady Susan, I trust you had no ill effects from your late night?" Hugh led her away from her cousin. Hugh had primed Elizabeth so she conversed with Jasper to his obvious annoyance.

"I always enjoy an assembly. Dancing is one of my favorite things to do." She looked as merry as a grig.

"And hiding valuable books? Is that another delight of yours?" Hugh scolded, knowing she would hate it.

"So?" She gave him a wary scowl. "I admitted that."

"I still do not understand how you could do that. That you could treat a valuable book in such a cavalier manner! You know how much my books mean to me."

"Obviously more than I do," she snapped, her temper flaring. Without Jasper to nudge her to silence, she went on. "So I hid that dratted book. I am tired of always being ignored. I believe I don't wish to marry you. Life with you would be a dead bore." With that satisfactory statement, she drew off her glove, removed the ring, and dropped it into Hugh's open hand.

He sighed. "I quite understand. You need someone else, someone more like your cousin."

She gave Hugh a narrow stare before turning to gaze at the devoted Jasper. She pulled on her glove, giving him a beckoning nod.

He caught her look and at once came to her side, smiling fondly at her. He'd made it clear that he would do anything for her. "You wish to leave now?"

"Yes. I have had quite enough of Latham Court and everyone in it." Head held high she made a grand exit worthy of a queen.

Hugh grinned at Elizabeth, who applauded.

"I congratulate you on the first step," she said, her eyes twinkling with mischief.

"What next?"

"Tabitha, of course."

Chapter Fifteen

Mary Ann Gower hailed Tabitha as she drove through Rustcombe on her way to Latham Court. It was a surprise to see the pretty chestnut-haired woman out and about so early on a Monday morn. She looked about to burst with news.

"I suppose you have heard the news," Mary Ann explained eagerly. "It is all over the village."

"I fear I have heard not a word of anything unusual," Tabitha replied.

"Well, I heard from our maid who is sister to a maid at the Court that Lady Susan has broken her engagement to Lord Latham! Seems he didn't pay her enough attention. *She* wanted to go gadding about and *he* likes his books." She paused a moment before thoughtfully adding, "Just as you do and Mr. Ainsworth does not."

"What an astute observation," Tabitha replied prudently, aware the groom who drove the gig could hear every word said. "Well, I am sorry that it had to come to this, but it is better that they discover now that they do not suit, rather than later. Think how frightful it would be to be wed to one who was not agreeable."

"Oh!" Mary Ann's eyes widened in speculation. "I daresay her father will send her to London next Season. She didn't take this past one." This was said with pious sympathy for Lady Susan. That young lady had not endeared herself to the local citizens in spite of her beauty and the charm she could offer when she pleased.

"Who can say? I'm certain that Lady Susan will have a fine future. Indeed, she may already have chosen her path." Like others, Tabitha wondered about Mr. West.

"I imagine you are anxious to return to your copying. Mr. Ainsworth is very understanding to permit you to work with his lordship." Mary Ann studied her with eyes that sought to pry information on the true nature of their engagement. "He does not seem to mind?"

Tabitha gave her a wry look. "Well, as to that, he said something about his not having to worry that I'd attract the attention of his lordship."

"Did he, now? How foolish of him. I fancy there are many men who would find your pale hair pleasing."

There was so much doubt in her voice that Tabitha was hard-pressed not to laugh. She waved farewell after murmuring to the groom that he could proceed.

The road to Latham Court wound through a pretty area with pretty plantings. The trip took just long enough for Tabitha to digest the news Mary Ann so eagerly imparted.

Just why that young woman was so anxious that Tabitha be aware of the change of his lordship's status from engaged to unattached was unclear. Before she could decide on a motive, Crowder was coming down the front steps to assist her from the carriage. Tabitha thanked the groom who had driven the gig, then walked inside with Crowder.

There was an air of suppressed excitement about the butler. Tabitha thought she could guess. He'd disliked Lady Susan and would not be sorry the engagement had ended.

"Would you care for some tea now or later, Miss Herbert?"

"Perhaps now? And is Miss Latham about? Or Lady Purcell?" Tabitha wondered what Elizabeth would have to say regarding the broken betrothal. She had not seemed fond of Lady Susan—nor had Miss Latham for that matter.

"There you are," Elizabeth caroled as she carefully came down the stairs. "There is such news this morning."

Remaining silent, for there was nothing more annoying than to have someone spoil momentous news by confessing it had already been heard, Tabitha smiled her greeting while trying to look properly curious.

Elizabeth hurried to take Tabitha's hand, leading her to the drawing room, tossing a polite request for tea over her shoulder as they went.

"You can guess what has pleased me if you wish."

"I am a terrible one to guess at anything," Tabitha confessed. "Just tell me what has happened, I beg you."

"Lady Susan broke the engagement yesterday! She declared that our dearest Hugh did not suit her—merely because he wouldn't dance to her tune."

"I daresay no man wants to be under a cat's paw. Your George isn't, is he? He seems a strong man."

"True." Elizabeth beamed, unconsciously stroking her burgeoning waistline. "But I must say that Hugh does not seem the slightest bit downcast. I heard him whistling earlier this morning." She gave Tabitha a meaningful look.

Crowder entered with a large tray bearing all that was necessary for morning tea, including light-as-a-feather scones. For a brief time all conversation was confined to comments on the tea and scones, and the weather.

"I saw Miss Gower as I passed through the village this morning," Tabitha said over the rim of her teacup.

"I trust you do not mind my saying this, but it is my opinion—confirmed by George—that she has her eye on Mr. Ainsworth." Elizabeth gave Tabitha a guarded look.

"Do you? Oh, I devoutly hope so," Tabitha murmured.

"He certainly seemed taken with her on Saturday night at the assembly. He asked her to dance three times!"

"That sounds promising, does it not?" Tabitha replied.

Before Elizabeth could reply to this delightful comment, Aunt Harriet bustled into the room. "Crowder assured me that more tea is on the way. I was about to have mine when I learned you have come, Tabitha. I fancy Elizabeth has told you the news? We are much relieved. I even suspect Hugh is as well." She exchanged a glance with her niece, one of enormous satisfaction. Crowder hurried in with a tray of tea things.

Nothing was said until the butler had left the room.

Elizabeth was fairly bursting with questions. When he was well out of hearing, she said, "You do not mind that your betrothed is enthralled with Miss Gower?"

"What's this? Mr. Ainsworth taken with another when he could have Tabitha!" Aunt Harriet set her cup down with a decided clink. "Oh, good. I am so glad. I trust you are not down pin over this. You truly are not well matched."

"So I have decided," Tabitha admitted dryly. "I

fancy he will be relieved when I inform him that we do not suit."

Elizabeth chuckled. "It would seem that the tangle is becoming unsnarled."

"We hope so. I wonder what Lady Susan will do now?" Aunt Harriet mused. "She is lovely, and can be kind."

"It would be too much to expect that elderly uncle who has been ailing for ages to finally pop off, leaving all that lovely money to Jasper." Elizabeth cast a quick look at Tabitha. "You are not drawn to *him*, are you?"

"Not in the slightest. But then, who could get to know him when he was Lady Susan's perpetual shadow?"

Aunt Harriet chuckled. "Oh, my dear, you do have a way with words."

"Who has a way with words?" Lord Latham inquired as he strode into the room. When he perceived that Tabitha was with his sister and aunt, he paused before continuing. "Good morning, Miss Herbert. Have you returned to work?" His expression was shuttered. Tabitha could detect nothing of whatever emotions that may simmer within him.

"It was my intention unless you have other plans?"

Hugh studied the lovely blonde seated so primly on the sofa with his sister. Elizabeth's eyes brimmed with mirth and he wondered what had been said before he entered the room. He had no doubt that the news of the broken betrothal had been offered to Tabitha. How had she reacted? And he also wondered if his sister had daringly offered comments on how badly Ainsworth had behaved at the assembly.

Since Crowder had apparently figured that his lordship might join the ladies, an extra teacup sat on the tray. Elizabeth poured, then offered the plate of scones.

"Whenever I must travel, I often think of Cook's scones. I doubt there are any better." He glanced at Tabitha, who was busy licking a crumb from her lips.

She rose from the sofa, giving him a hesitant look. "If it is agreeable with you, I shall go to the library now. You said there was a stack of pages waiting for me."

"There isn't any rush now, is there? You aren't about to hurry off to marry your squire?"

The shock in her eyes almost made him laugh.

"No!" She tossed Elizabeth a look, then hurried from the drawing room as though chased by myriad mice.

In the silence of the library Tabitha could calm her racing heart. What would Lord Latham say when Elizabeth told him that she intended to end her betrothal? Most likely he would make some polite rejoinder. After all, merely because he had kissed her was no reason that she could expect anything more. Foolish girl.

Tabitha was well into the first of the pages when Lord Latham came. She gave him a cautious look, then turned her gaze to the paper upon which she carefully transcribed his scribbling.

"It is good to have you back here. I have missed your silent presence while working on the translation."

She chuckled. "My silence? Oh, I think hardly that." To be appreciated for her silence was rather daunting.

"You are peaceful. *You* do not demand I take you someplace, nor complain about my reading books." He paced back and forth before the fireplace, looking ill-treated.

"And why should I? In the first place, I do not expect you to take me anyplace. And secondly, I love to read, so I could scarce complain if you do. What odd comments, if I may be so bold? I suspect you are annoyed at something."

"You don't have any headache? Or suffer any after-effects of your ordeal?" He wandered closer to where she sat, admiring her neat coil of silver gilt hair. It had a few tendrils to either side of her face, softening any attempt at severity. Her bonnet must have disarranged them. She looked her usual lovable self in her demure lilac gown with its treble ruff of delicate lace.

She shook her head. "None. I'm sorry to learn your engagement has been ended. At least, I presume I must offer my sympathy. You do not have the look of a broken man." She cast a side-glance at him, looking as though she repressed a grin that longed to break forth.

Hugh wondered if she was remotely aware how flirtatious her little glance had been. Those lovely blue eyes revealed more than she evidently realized. "Elizabeth told me you intend to end your betrothal to Mr. Ainsworth. May I inquire what prompted this? Possibly his behavior at the assembly in Tonbridge?"

She stiffened and he feared he had intruded too far.

"It would never do," she confessed in a quiet voice. "His love for horses and dogs don't agree with my love for books and flowers." She gave him a dry look. "Miss Gower has a fondness for horses and dogs besides an ample dowry." She paused for a few moments before adding, "And I fear his mother would never accept me. I believe I should rather be a spinster than have to live with Mrs. Ainsworth."

"Let us hope that Miss Gower will be able to adapt to Mrs. Ainsworth. I hadn't intended to discuss it with you, but now it is mentioned, he behaved disgracefully at the assembly. He hovered over her like a bee over a flower in bloom, one from which he fully intended to sip."

"Yes, I saw that. You invited me to dance and that was kind of you, particularly when he so pointedly ignored me."

"Kindness had nothing to do with my asking you to dance," he said with deliberation.

She looked ready to run away, so Hugh walked over to his desk. "Shall we go on?"

He heard her sigh and smiled, albeit a trifle grimly.

Tabitha hoped the blaze of color in her cheeks died quickly. It had been somewhat mortifying when Sam had neglected her for the charms of Miss Gower. Small wonder that Mary Ann had studied her with such inquisitive eyes this morning. Well, it was what Tabitha had wanted for some time, so why did it hurt when Sam so obviously tumbled for another? It was not hurt, precisely. Perhaps pique was a better choice of a word.

The baron cleared his throat. Tabitha turned her attention to the page before her, dipping her pen into the pot of black ink.

Little was said the rest of the morning. She lunched with Aunt Harriet, Elizabeth, and George. When Harriet murmured something about dear Hugh going off on errands all the way to Tunbridge Wells, Tabitha suspected she'd not see him the rest of the day, nor did she.

Lord Latham returned the following day, saying nothing about what he had done or what errands had taken him so long. Not that Tabitha thought she deserved an accounting of his trip. She was interested. That was all.

He came into the library an hour after she had arrived and was settled at her task. "Good morning."

He checked the pages she had done and what remained. "I suggest you take a day off tomorrow. No doubt you have a few things you wish to do? I shall be busy. We can catch up the following day."

Feeling snubbed for some stupid reason, Tabitha merely nodded. "As you wish, sir."

"Elizabeth and George are leaving early next week. I am giving a dinner on Saturday. Will you come?"

"Of course, I will. I shall miss your sister very much. She is a darling person—so warm and charming."

"Our entire family is like that, you know." He looked as though he wanted to laugh and restrained himself.

"So I have been told." She would not respond to his provocation. It was tempting, though.

"You do not seem to believe me. Am I not warm and charming?" His dark eyes seemed to sparkle with an inner pleasure. It was like he knew something she ought to know and didn't and wanted to tease her about it. Unlikely!

Tabitha didn't think she wanted to answer that query. She looked pointedly at her desk, then back up at him. His gaze was fastened on her with an intensity that she found almost disturbing. "Sir?"

He came over to lean on her desk, staring down into her eyes. "What would you like to do if you could do anything you want? Anything in the world?"

Tabitha gulped, suddenly aware that more than anything in the world she wanted this gentleman who teased her, smiled at her, shared so much with her.

"I . . . I cannot say," she stammered.

"I wonder," he mused.

To her vast relief he did not pursue the matter, leaving the library at once. He muttered something about seeing his bailiff as he went out the door.

In the hallway, Hugh paused, thankful he had left

the library before succumbing to the strong desire to take Tabitha Herbert in his arms and likely shock her with his kiss. It would be no tame salute, not once he had that delicious little blonde where she belonged.

He would be glad when she spoke to Ainsworth. There could be no consideration of a union between himself and the lovely Tabitha until this mess was cleared up. How could two reasonably sensible people fall into such a tangle? Impetuosity was not one of his character traits.

The following morning seemed flat, dull. Tabitha assisted her mother around the house, then set off on a walk. She was restless, wanting something she couldn't have. She reached the small copse on the far edge of the glebe. Her father was fortunate that he was given such fine acreage along with the rectory. Mama had her fancy hens and a neat little orchard as well as the fields her father let out. They brought in a tidy sum to the family coffers.

Perching on the fence, she contemplated what she knew she must do, and dreaded doing. Fate took a hand when it presented none other than Sam Ainsworth coming in her direction on one of his prize chestnuts.

When he came abreast of her, he stopped, dismounted and joined her by the fence. "You are not at the Court today."

"No, I wasn't needed. Were you headed to the village?"

"I wanted to talk with you."

"Oh." She summoned her nerve, then continued. "I wanted to see you as well. Mr. Ainsworth, you did me great honor when you asked me to be your wife, but now I must tell you that I believe we would not suit."

The mixture of expressions that flitted across his

face was almost amusing. At first he looked affronted. After all, he was considered quite a catch, even for a rector's daughter. But then, Tabitha could tell when he realized he would be free to pursue the lovely Mary Ann Gower, no longer tied to Tabitha. He seemed pleased.

"I believe you will agree with me that our tastes are too dissimilar. I like to read and do not care for horses." That she had never been given the opportunity to like the beasts, not having a chance to learn to ride, was not mentioned.

"True. True," he answered eagerly. "My mother has raised a few doubts as well," he admitted.

"I can imagine." Tabitha just barely refrained from grimacing at the thought of what Mrs. Ainsworth must have said to her only son regarding his choice of a future wife.

"You want to end the betrothal." He stated the fact as though he wished to get it straight in his mind.

"You have the right of it. It isn't as though either of us were madly in love, or something like that." She withdrew the simple gold promise ring he had given her, offering it to Sam.

He accepted it with a frown, looking at the ring as though unhappy with the plainness of it. "True."

Tabitha felt strong irritation with the man. He didn't have to be quite so happy to be rid of her. Sam would never be given to pretence.

"That is that, then." She jumped down from the fence. She twisted her ankle in so doing, for a pain shot up her leg. She clamped her jaw shut, but Sam saw her distress.

"Now what did you do? I never did see such a female for getting herself into trouble." He picked her up in his arms to stare down at her. "I'll take you home."

Before he could put her on his horse, someone came rattling past in a smart curricle. Lord Latham! Tabitha closed her eyes in disgust. Now that she had ended the betrothal and was free of Sam, what should happen but that the baron see her in Sam's arms! She had not the slightest doubt his lordship had spotted them.

"Take me home, Sam. My ankle is horrid." She blinked back tears of pain and frustration.

"Best get a compress on it first thing." He placed her on the horse, then made excellent time back to the house where her mother took over at once. If she promptly spotted the lack of the promise ring, she said nothing about it.

"Thank you, Mr. Ainsworth. A soaking in my special salts will have her better in no time." He was dismissed.

Once Tabitha was in her room and her foot in the tub of water containing her mother's own remedy, her mother said, "You returned the ring and broke the engagement."

"I did. But when I went to jump down from the fence where I'd been sitting, my ankle gave way. Sam complained he had never seen a female for getting herself into trouble like I do. But I don't. Do I? These were accidents and they do happen."

"Of course, dear. Now rest your foot and don't you dare try to walk on it. I shall return directly."

"Mama," Tabitha added, "the baron went by just after Sam had picked me up." She made a wry face.

"So he observed you in Sam's arms?" At her daughter's sad nod, Mrs. Herbert merely smiled serenely. "Do not worry. All will come about in the end."

When alone, Tabitha stared at her wretched ankle before wiping a tear that insisted on trailing down her cheek. She sniffed. Well, she had said she would rather be a spinster than marry Sam Ainsworth and it looked as though that would be the case. It just proved that one should be more careful about what one said.

A message was sent to the Court regarding Tabitha's accident. No reply was forthcoming. Tabitha was certain she had burned every bridge from here to London and back.

Elizabeth came to see her the next day, bringing a bouquet of flowers. She looked at the swollen ankle and shook her head. "I am so sorry. When Hugh told us you had been injured I thought it a disaster, for he looked so grim."

"I shall not be able to make my way up to the house for a time. Someone would have to carry me everywhere, and that would be tedious." She gave her ankle an unhappy look.

"It should be as right as rain before you know it."

"Have you heard anything about Lady Susan?"

"Not her directly, but news regarding Jasper has come. Would you believe that elderly uncle actually died? And he left his considerable fortune to his nephew who bears his name? I suspect that Lady Susan and her perpetual shadow will be married as soon as the banns can be called."

"Well, it is likely for the best. Can you imagine any husband tolerating Jasper underfoot forever?"

Elizabeth laughed, then observed, "I see you are not wearing that little promise ring anymore. Dare I inquire as to the reason?"

"I told Sam we would not suit. He seemed quite happy."

"What a nodcock. Oh, I am to remind you that you must come to the dinner Saturday. We are counting on you to be there."

"I shall be sorry to see you leave." Tabitha gave Elizabeth a warm smile. "I hope all will go well with you, and the next time I see you there will be healthy babes in your arms."

"Of that, I am confident. All the women in our family have healthy babies. I will, too."

Tabitha envied her not a little. Spinsterhood seemed terribly bleak at the moment.

Chapter Sixteen

Hugh felt as though his world had fallen apart. The sight of Tabitha Herbert in Sam Ainsworth's arms made him furious. He wanted nothing more than to growl at everyone.

She had indicated she would break with Sam and there she was, in his arms. Hugh had wanted to stop and snatch her from Ainsworth's clasp, then proceed to read her a scold before kissing her until she was breathless. Never in his life had he imagined such frustration!

He had finally freed himself from Lady Susan. An honorable man didn't jilt a lady. Although if pressed, Hugh would not have actually wed the chit. Not after knowing Tabitha. Honor went just so far—at least in his mind.

But that Tabitha Herbert would say she intended to break with Ainsworth, then be seen in his arms had cut Hugh to the quick. He wanted to make her his wife—and she was flirting with Sam! He took another turn before the fireplace where he had been pacing slowly back and forth for some time. It was an utterly exasperating situation.

"You, dear brother, are vexing." Elizabeth gave him an annoyed look from where she curled up on the sofa.

Hugh shook his head, but ceased his pacing.

George added, "You feel thwarted? I recall often feeling like that when younger and single."

Hugh glared at him, wondering if he had endured anything remotely like this when courting Elizabeth.

"I went to see Tabitha this afternoon." Elizabeth spoke to the room in general. "I shall call on her again tomorrow." At an arrested look from Hugh, she went on. "Did I not tell you that the poor dear injured her ankle? Lucky for her Mr. Ainsworth was handy to cart her home. She won't be able to write tomorrow. She is confined in bed. It is too bad—to have a day off, then be injured! Her ankle is badly swollen! Had you been at home when her note came, I'd have told you. I was gone when you returned."

The anger drained from Hugh. Had he not been so stupidly jealous he should have suspected something of the sort. He should have known that Tabitha was far too honest to behave in such a manner. She was not one to deceive!

"That poor child has had a dreadful assortment of accidents of late," Aunt Harriet observed. "The most dreadful was the attack by that nasty swan. Be sure you take her some flowers. Perhaps I will join you. I am fond of the girl. What a contrast she is to some others." Harriet bestowed an admonishing look on her nephew.

Hugh roused himself. "Aunt, request some strawberries from the gardener as well as the flowers. As I recall, she likes strawberries."

"I don't suppose you would like to join us?"

"Visiting the ill and injured is women's work." Much as he longed to see her, he didn't want his sister and aunt present at the time!

"You certainly spent enough time with her after she was attacked by that swan," Aunt Harriet riposted.

"But perhaps she doesn't wish to see you. After ending her betrothal she might be feeling a trifle down pin."

"I doubt that, Aunt," Elizabeth denied. "When we spoke of it, she said they would never have suited. For example, Tabitha never had a chance to learn to ride. Mr. Ainsworth, dunce that he is, never thought to teach her. I trust her next suitor will not be so half-witted." She glanced again at Hugh before turning to her book.

Hugh gave George a long-suffering look.

George, in response, rose from his chair. "Come with me, will you, Hugh? I saw something in the barn I think may need tending."

Grateful for any sort of reprieve, Hugh joined George. They left the two women to the peace of the drawing room.

"What is it?" Hugh inquired as they quitted the house.

"Nothing. I recognized a fellow in distress. Elizabeth can try the patience of a saint at times."

"I totally misread what I saw while coming home yesterday. Makes me feel like an utter fool."

"Well, if that is the worst of it, it isn't too bad."

"It's that obvious?" Hugh said with dismay.

"Only to one who has been in the same spot."

The two men sauntered down to the barn, cementing a relationship that had grown since his sister's wedding.

When Aunt Harriet entered Tabitha's pretty bedroom the next afternoon she carried a lovely bouquet of flowers. Elizabeth followed with a bowl of strawberries.

"Hugh ordered the berries for you." Elizabeth

grinned. She placed the bowl on the bedside table. The berries were large and ripe with droplets of water on them. Tabitha popped one in her mouth at Elizabeth's urging.

"Flowers and berries!" She licked her lips. "How very nice." She attempted to be casual with her query. "And how does his lordship go on? With the translating, I mean." Tabitha wondered if she'd ever acquire the polish that let a woman be offhand when speaking of the man she loved.

"Actually, I don't think he has done much. He went out with George this morning and they have yet to return."

"How are you feeling, my dear?" Aunt Harriet inquired.

Tabitha gestured to her ankle propped on a fat pillow. "The swelling is going down and the pain is less."

Elizabeth smiled. "Look at it this way, you have now put all the stupid things you can do in a lifetime behind you. Henceforth you can only be brilliant."

"How I wish that might be." Tabitha turned her head toward the door after hearing a rustle of skirts.

Mary Ann Gower entered the room, carrying a cluster of pretty garden flowers. She paused when she saw the ladies from the great house and showed a reluctance to enter.

"Come in," Tabitha said and made the introductions.

"I am so sorry you were hurt. When I chatted with Mrs. Ainsworth at the village store she mentioned that you'd had an accident." Mary Ann glanced at the other visitors, then added, "She also told me that you ended your betrothal."

"That is true enough. It was providential that Mr. Ainsworth was close by when I fell. He brought me home." Tabitha exchanged a look with Elizabeth. "He took the termination of our engagement very well, I thought."

Mrs. Herbert entered with a vase for the flowers. While there, she inspected Tabitha's ankle, poking gently at the swelling. "It is down some. I believe you will be able to go out for dinner come Saturday."

Mary Ann revealed her curiosity, her eyes questioning.

Elizabeth graciously answered her unspoken query. "My husband and I are leaving early next week. My brother insists on having a dinner before we go. I wished Tabitha be invited, for she has become a dear friend to me."

"I heard that Lady Susan and her cousin Mr. West are to be married. How very odd, when so recently she was engaged . . ." Mary Ann broke off in confusion as she realized the connection of Elizabeth to the former fiancé.

"We approve of her marriage," Aunt Harriet added. "Jasper is ever at her side and will be a good husband."

"Perhaps there will be other marriages in the village this summer?" Elizabeth suggested, fixing her gaze on Mary Ann. "What do you think?"

Mary Ann turned deep red and murmured something about having to get home. She fled around the corner after making a hasty farewell.

Mrs. Herbert hurried after her.

"I didn't mean to send your caller away. However, I think you are tired." Elizabeth came to stand by the bed, taking Tabitha's hand in hers. "You must come to dinner. Hugh won't be fit to live with if you don't." With that interesting comment, she added her farewell.

Aunt Harriet kissed Tabitha on the cheek and admonished her to enjoy the berries. "They are very fine."

Tabitha felt well enough to be up and about before Saturday. She had her father drive her up to the Court on Thursday so she might catch up on the copying. Mama had wrapped a strip of linen around her foot so that it felt comfortable as long as she didn't try to walk too far.

Using the cane her father had found, she made her way to the front door. When Crowder opened it to discover her waiting, his welcome was most gratifying.

"I can't do a reel or a jig, but I believe I can sit quietly and write." She made her way to the library.

Lord Latham was at his desk. He glanced up in surprise as she entered the room, then rose to hurry to her side. "I didn't expect to see you today. Are you certain you feel up to writing?"

Tabitha flashed a look at him before fixing her gaze on the floor. "I am quite well, thank you. A mere tenderness is all that remains. I ought to know better than to jump from a fence that high onto uneven ground."

At the little writing desk where she had worked all this time, she stopped, then turned to face him.

An awkward silence ensued. The clock in the far end of the room ticked loudly. The rustling of the oak outside the window intruded on their peace. Yet there was tension between them. It seemed tangible. Tabitha thought she could almost see it. She searched his face for clues to his feelings.

"Tabitha . . ." He seemed at a loss for words.

"You know I ended my betrothal to Mr. Ainsworth." She held up her hand, with the lack of a ring evident. He took her slim hand in his capable one.

"I was glad to hear that. He does not deserve you."

She grimaced, leaning more on her cane. As much as she longed to stand speaking with him, her ankle protested.

He swept her into his arms, startling her completely. "I can't have you swooning on me. I think once was enough." His smile lit his brown eyes with golden lights.

Tabitha leaned her head against his shoulder. It was a marvelous place to be—in his arms. She met his eyes as he gazed down at her. He began to lower his head toward her. She leaned toward him to accept his kiss. She would feel the wondrous touch of his lips on her again. She could scarce wait. It might even be better!

The rattle of crockery heralded the arrival of tea. Crowder, followed by Aunt Harriet bustled into the room.

All at once Tabitha found herself tenderly placed on the armchair by the little desk.

"We shall continue this interesting scene at a more private moment," the baron said softly for her ears alone.

Drat! She knew he had been about to kiss her. Why did Crowder choose this moment to bring in the blasted tea!

"Good morning, Miss Latham." She'd be polite if it killed her. Her smile at the lady was a trifle strained.

"Since when have I become Miss Latham? Aunt Harriet, if you please, dear girl. I shall pour, Crowder."

Tabitha accepted her teacup with every evidence of one who is dying of thirst. She met the baron's wry expression with an equally dry one of her own.

"I trust I did not interrupt anything?" Harriet asked, ignoring the look from her nephew.

Tabitha decided that Aunt Harriet meant to chaperon to the hilt. The baron's eyes promised that the time would come when they could talk . . . and perhaps more.

So, she endured polite conversation and drank two cups of tea. She made suitable comments on plans for the farewell dinner. Regarding the news about Lady Susan and Jasper West, she observed, "It is indeed a blessing that he would inherit all that money just when it was most needed."

They were given no moments alone the rest of the day. Tabitha sensed the baron was as annoyed as she, but little could be done about it. He insisted upon taking her home.

When they arrived at her house it was all hustle and bustle. Giving Hugh a bewildered look, Tabitha allowed him to carry her inside, then set her on her feet.

"What is going on?" she demanded of her mother as she whirled past with an armload of clothes, freshly washed and pressed. It wasn't Monday.

"We are to leave at once. A letter came from Nympha. She is to marry Lord Nicholas next week and we must be there!" She rushed up the stairs, leaving Tabitha standing in the hall feeling as though her world just fell apart.

"I gather this rules out the dinner on Saturday. Tell Elizabeth good-bye for me. Give her my kiss." Tabitha stared at Hugh. To be parted from him now was cruel.

"I will be here when you return. This doesn't alter anything between us. Does it?" He looked anxious.

She shook her head. "No, of course not." She held out her hand, which he took in his. They stood there in silence, staring at one another. Tabitha wondered if her eyes spoke to him as his did to her.

Hugh glanced around, and seeing no one, bent and bestowed an all-too-brief kiss on Tabitha's lips. "I'll see you as soon as you return."

She watched his shiny black curricle until it was a speck in the distance. Only then did she make her way up the stairs to her room.

The traveling coach sent for them was spacious, but the route north to Nottingham seemed to go on forever. Eventually they turned off the main road, just before the village of Mansfield. This led to an imposing mansion, far larger than any of them had expected.

Nympha, alerted to their arrival, rushed from the house to greet them, with hugs and kisses for all. Behind her Lord Nicholas and a slender gray-haired woman followed. Mrs. Herbert greeted her aunt with a fond embrace. They all trouped into the elegant home with the promise of a late dinner. Priscilla popped up to surprise them, having driven up with Mercy Herbert and Lord Latimer, Priscilla's betrothed! They had picked up Drusilla, so nearly all the family was here. Only Claudia was absent. Tabitha studied Lord Latimer, liking what she saw in him.

"This is sudden, I know, but we simply did not wish to wait." Nympha exchanged a look with her mother, darting a glance at Great-aunt Mrs. Coxmoor, then back to her mother.

Tabitha, not entirely dense, figured that the elderly lady was none too strong and that Nympha wished to be married before something happened to her great-aunt.

Another surprise came when Priscilla asked Nympha if she would be willing to share her day! Felix had a special license and they wished to marry at once. Since the chapel was ready and their father inclined to agree, Nympha was thrilled to share the ceremony with Priscilla.

When at last the four sisters were alone in the fine room assigned to Tabitha, they had a chance to talk.

"Who would have thought you would marry Lord Nicholas?" Tabitha said with a gurgle of laughter. "I can recall when you detested the man."

"True. He is wonderful, and perfect for me!" Nympha frowned at her youngest sister. "You have had a time of it, what with helping Lord Latham with his translation, then being attacked by a horrid swan. Did I see you limping when you entered the house? What now?"

"I was sitting on the glebe fence when I told Sam Ainsworth I couldn't marry him. I jumped down and twisted my ankle." She casually added, "I've spent a lot of time at Latham Court."

"With the Black Baron! I do not believe it!" Priscilla cried, then burst into laughter.

"He is far from horrid! He is the kindest, most caring man in the world." Tabitha gave them a misty smile.

Dru shook her head. "Who would have thought it? I confess I am glad you are not to marry Sam. Think of living with his mother!"

Tabitha shuddered dramatically.

"There is something else, I think," Nympha prompted.

"I have fallen in love with the baron."

"I thought he was engaged to Lady Susan," Dru said.

"That is all in the past. Priscilla?" Tabitha asked. "I had no idea that you are to wed Lord Latimer. How lovely! I began to suspect something was in the air from your letters. And how nice of Nympha to share her day."

Drusilla grinned, inserting, "Well, I am to marry my dear Adrian come autumn. So soon we will all be wed. You will, too, Tabitha. Just wait and see."

It was late when the sisters caught up on all their news. When they eventually went to bed, three had happy hearts, the other nurtured hopes for her future.

The wedding was quite as splendid as anyone might wish. Mr. Herbert, resplendent in his clerical garb, gave away his daughters to their fine gentlemen. Pailthorpe Chapel bloomed with bouquets of flowers as well as happy smiles.

Tabitha, Drusilla, and Adam sat with their mother and Mrs. Coxmoor while they viewed the double ceremony. Later they waved off the happy couples following a splendid wedding breakfast.

The Herberts remained a few days, enjoying the time with Mrs. Coxmoor and Aunt Mercy Herbert.

When it came time to leave, Tabitha packed ells of gorgeous lace in hope it would turn a simple silk dress into an elegant wedding gown.

Only Tabitha remained a spinster. She had faith that things would work out, but so much could happen in the weeks she was away. While she was pleased to see her sisters and attend the ceremony she longed to be with the baron.

"Think on it, dear," Mrs. Herbert mused to her husband on their way to Rustcombe. "One daughter married to the younger son of a marquis, another wed to an earl, the third engaged to my dear friend's son, the Marquess of Brentford. Claudia's baronet has a handsome home. God has surely blessed our family. Only Tabitha remains."

"And Adam, of course," Mr. Herbert added.

"Indeed. He has years before he can think of settling down." They both stared at Tabitha until she wished she might ride outside with Adam.

How could she tell them she longed to marry Baron Latham? He had made no promises. That farewell kiss may have been nothing more than that—a farewell kiss.

The rain that had held off the day they arrived home, poured down in earnest the following morning. Tabitha peered out of her window, feeling as gloomy as the weather.

"A young lady to see you, miss. Says her name is Miss Gower." The maid bobbed a curtsy, leaving the door open behind her as she returned to her work.

Tabitha hurried down to the sitting room. What could have brought Mary Ann Gower out on such a dreadful day! She greeted her with a certain amount of reserve.

"You will think me daft to be out in this rain, but I had to see you before anyone else spoke to you about it."

Tabitha's heart plunged to her toes. Something had happened to the baron. Oh, pray it was not too dreadful!

Mary Ann hesitated while Tabitha waited in suspense.

"What is it, Mary Ann?" Tabitha asked when the silence went on far too long.

"I am to marry Mr. Ainsworth," she blurted. "We have everything in common and I care for him very much. I know you broke your engagement, but I trust this is not a terrible shock." She gave Tabitha a worried look.

"I wish you the very best, both of you." Tabitha suspected her color was rushing back. The relief she felt was so great she could scarce speak.

Mary Ann dutifully inquired about the trip and the wedding, her eyes widening as she heard of the double ceremony for Nympha and Priscilla, plus Drusilla's plans to wed a marquis in autumn. "My goodness!"

Tabitha smiled. "Many changes for us. I am the spinster of the family, I guess."

Mary Ann bestowed a pitying look on her, but merely curtsied before making her farewell.

When the rain ceased, Tabitha donned her pelisse, bonnet and gloves. "I am going up to the Court, Mama. I might as well return to work."

She ignored her mother's speculative look. Papa drove the gig, dropping her off prior to his parish calls.

Crowder greeted her with restraint. Tabitha began to worry. What had occurred while she was gone? She hurried into the library. She soon settled down with the pile of papers. It didn't appear to have grown much. She wondered what Hugh had been doing.

"So you are back," the object of her thoughts said as he strode into the room and up to where she sat.

He placed his hands on the desk and leaned over her, yet he wasn't the least menacing. Her hopes rose from her toes to somewhere in her midsection.

"Tabitha. It has been an eternity! I will not have it again! You hear?" He walked around to pluck her from her chair and pull her tightly to him. "I can't take the separation, my love. Never again! If ever you must go somewhere, we will go together."

She touched his face, stroking his cheek with loving fingers. "Truly? And how will this come about?"

He kissed her with all the pent-up desire that had grown while they were apart. When he finally drew back to gaze at her with adoring eyes. "You will marry me. Then we will always be together, my dearest."

How like the man not to ask but to announce. "I believe that might be managed, my love. It is customary to ask, but I won't insist on that."

He grimaced, rather comically, she thought. He took

a fine sapphire ring from his inner pocket to slip on her finger. "Now you are almost mine." He gathered her tightly to him again, his kiss entirely satisfactory.

"Oh, good," Aunt Harriet pronounced from the doorway. "Now I can help plan your wedding."

Tabitha and Hugh turned to look at her.

"Crowder is bringing tea, but I think I'll tell him to open champagne instead. We must celebrate!"

Author's Note

Mute swans are usually very mild-mannered and considered semi-domesticated. However, they are strongly territorial and adopt a threatening posture when faced with an intruder. An explosive grunting call usually accompanies this posture. In spite of this territorial inclination a mute swam will often show no fear of humans—at least when not nesting—even to the point of taking food from outstretched hands. When researching for this book I came across the account of a woman who was attacked by a swan, dragged into the nearby lake and nearly drowned. The woman was hospitalized with minor injuries.

So, while it is unusual for a swan to attack, it is not unheard of for them to attack a human.